H

P

H ... rs
that his well cut suit cannot conceal. But for the broken nose, a legacy of an early battle in the boxing ring, he would be as handsome as he is massive . . .

He is always jumping in with both feet where the police fear to tread. And no thief, blackmailer or murderer ever comes up against a tougher, more resourceful, deadlier enemy than

PATRICK DAWLISH

THE LONG SEARCH, one of the Patrick Dawlish series, is by John Creasey writing as Gordon Ashe, of which there are now over forty titles and many have been published by Corgi Books.

Born in 1908, John Creasey died in June 1973. Overall, his books have sold nearly a hundred million copies and have been translated into 28 languages.

As well as travelling extensively, he had a particular interest in politics and was the founder of *All Party Alliance*, which advocates a new system of government by the best candidates from all parties and independents. He fought in five parliamentary by-elections for the movement.

Also by JOHN CREASEY

FIND THE BODY
FIRST A MURDER
RUN AWAY TO MURDER
DON'T LET HIM KILL
THE BLACK SPIDERS
DEATH IN THE TREES
THE CRIMEHATERS
DEATH IN A HURRY
DAY OF FEAR
ELOPE TO DEATH
ROGUE'S RANSOM
DEATH FROM BELOW
SLEEPY DEATH
NO NEED TO DIE
THE SNATCH
THE BIG CALL
THE MAN WHO STAYED ALIVE
THE SPEAKER
KILL OR BE KILLED
GIVE ME MURDER
WAIT FOR DEATH
COME HOME TO DEATH
BLACK FOR THE BARON
MISSING OR DEAD
A PROMISE OF DIAMONDS
THE BARON RETURNS
A ROPE FOR THE BARON
A BRANCH FOR THE BARON
BLAME FOR THE BARON
TRAP THE BARON
DEATH ON DEMAND
SHADOW THE BARON
A TASTE OF TREASURE
TERROR BY DAY
DEATH IN DIAMONDS
MURDER TOO LATE
DOUBLE FOR DEATH
A CASE FOR THE BARON
THE DARK CIRCLE
THE BARON AGAIN
A CLUTCH OF COPPERS
INVITATION TO ADVENTURE
DEATH ON THE MOVE
REWARD FOR THE BARON
ENGAGEMENT WITH DEATH
WARN THE BARON
SHADOW OF DEATH
VERSUS THE BARON
BARK MYSTERY
THE TOFF TAKES SHARES
THE TOFF ON BOARD
A KNIFE FOR THE TOFF
MEET THE BARON
CLOSE THE DOOR ON MURDER
THE TOFF IS BACK
A PUZZLE IN PEARLS
TWO MEN MISSING
MURDER WITH MUSHROOMS
A SCREAM OF MURDER
ACCUSE THE TOFF
THE TOFF AMONG THE MILLIONS
KILL THE TOFF
THE GALLOWS ARE WAITING
'WARE DANGER
ATTACK THE BARON
THE SECRET MURDER
HUNT THE TOFF
THE BARON AT LARGE
ALIAS THE BARON
MYSTERY MOTIVE
A RABBLE OF REBELS
LET'S KILL UNCLE LIONEL
CALL FOR THE BARON
MURDER MOST FOUL
DEATH IN FLAMES
DEATH IN HIGH PLACES
THE BARON COMES BACK
THE BARON AND THE BEGGAR
THE BARON RETURNS
THE TOFF AT BUTLIN'S

and published by CORGI BOOKS

John Creasey
writing as Gordon Ashe

The Long Search

CORGI BOOKS
A DIVISION OF TRANSWORLD PUBLISHERS LTD

THE LONG SEARCH
A CORGI BOOK 0 552 09511 7

Originally published in Great Britain by
John Long Limited

PRINTING HISTORY
John Long edition published 1953
Corgi edition published 1963
Corgi edition reissued 1974

This book is set in Monotype Times

Corgi Books are published by Transworld Publishers Ltd.,
Cavendish House, 57-59 Uxbridge Road,
Ealing, London, W.5.
Made and printed in Great Britain by
Hunt Barnard Printing Ltd., Aylesbury, Bucks.

Contents

CHAPTER I

THE BIG MAN

HE was a big man and he looked as if he carried a load of trouble. That showed in his tired eyes and the tightness of his full lips. He walked slowly, almost stiffly, from his Buick convertible towards the Canyon's rim. The Canyon was hidden from him until he was close to the rim. Other people were looking, but he did not seem to notice them.

The Canyon came slowly into his view. First, the tops of mountains on a level with his eyes; then the giant formations, the mountain ranges, the gorges and deep valleys, the pale reds and mauves, browns, blues and yellows, each colour laying a million years bare to the winds. Shadows, mistily grey, moved slowly across the still, silent vastness, as small white clouds drifted across the face of the sun; when one was gone, another took its place, and each shadow changed each colour that it fell upon.

Although he was so big, the Canyon dwarfed the man; had there been a hundred thousand, all giants, it would have dwarfed them. The few who stood and looked into the silent depth spoke in muted voices; two turned away abruptly, as if they could not bear to contemplate the scene a moment longer. The big man went closer to the stone wall, his tired bloodshot eyes roving, as if he sought to see beyond the mountains and through the rocks of ages.

Silence rose out of the Canyon, until, after a long while, a voice came with it. In fact there was no voice except the one in his mind; clear, dear, precious; but he could hear it, whereas he could not hear the voices of the people near him, or the sounds of cars moving in and out of the car park behind him.

The voice said:

"*It's fantastic, Pat, you can hear the silence. Does that seem silly? You can, though.*"

The big man listened and heard the silence which came out of the earth and the mountains below him. It seemed to take possession of him, as he knew that it must have taken possession of her. A man and his wife who meant much to each other saw many things through the same eyes, heard much through the same ears, saw clearly what others could not see.

Her voice faded; he didn't hear it again.

He turned, and with his back to the Canyon, stared at the hotel with its log walls and big windows, some overlooking the Canyon. He needed sleep, looked as if without it he would drop. The power in his big body was numbed with weariness; each step seemed an effort. He went slowly up the wooden steps to the verandah, where a few people sat and where two Hopi Indians stood, wearing white tunics with purple sashes, dark hair sleek and long and ribboned, broad, copper-hued faces expressionless.

Inside, the hotel was cool, and gave an impression of spaciousness. Two people were buying postcards at the cigar and candy store, another buying cigarettes. The reception-desk was opposite, and a young room clerk looked up at the big man invitingly.

"Help you, sir?"

"I telephoned for a room. My name is Dawlish."

Anyone observing the big man would have been sure that he wasn't American; Scandinavian, perhaps, with his corn-coloured hair and fair complexion, although his clothes, not his looks, betrayed his foreignness. His voice placed him at once; he was English.

"Yes, Mr. Dawlch." The room clerk busied himself briefly, and then looked up. "That's right, we've the room you asked for—119." He showed no curiosity because Dawlish had asked for a particular room. "Where's your baggage, Mr. Dawlch?" He had pushed a form across the counter.

"In my car." Dawlish filled in the details slowly, deliberately, and wrote the number of his car in a corner, then took the car key from his pocket and put it on top of the form. "It's in the car park, there's the number. A Buick convertible. Nothing in the boot."

"In the——?"

"Sorry. Trunk," Dawlish said, and looked as if he were too tired to think. "Please send up some sandwiches, and a Scotch-and-soda. As quickly as you can."

"It's on the way, Mr. Dawlch. I'll have a boy show you to your room." The clerk glanced up commandingly, and a silent Hopi came soft-footed, to take the key and lead the way up the stairs, half-way round a circular landing, then along a passage to a small room with a double bed and a window which overlooked a yard. Dawlish, almost stupid, put a quarter into the hand which had made no inviting move. The door closed. Dawlish took himself to the window and looked out upon several cars, a paved yard, and one wing of the hotel. Men were talking, a radio was on.

No woman spoke, but Dawlish heard a woman's voice.

"*I've a little back room,* 119, *but I'm glad it doesn't overlook the Canyon. I don't think I could bear to look into that every time I came to the window.*"

He turned. The double bed was the bed his wife had slept on. It had one pillow, as it would have had for her just twenty-eight days ago. It stood on polished boards of pale pine, and there was a faint, fresh smell of pine. The writing-table in a corner near him was the same wood; his wife had probably sat at that and written the letter through which she now talked to him.

"*There's a guide named Bill—I think he's called a Ranger—and it's one of those absurd coincidences, darling, he married a girl from Haslemere, I'm going to see her this evening.*"

Dawlish's wife, Felicity, had come nearly six thousand miles and talked to a guide named Bill, who had married an English girl from the Dawlish home town, in Surrey. Felicity would have been delighted; Dawlish could imagine the eagerness with which she had gone out to see Bill's wife. She had never written to say how she had got on, there had been no other letter; only silence, a silence as deep and as hurtful as that which came out of the Canyon.

Dawlish went into the bathroom, ran the cold tap, doused his face and felt the welcome relief of the shock of the cold water. He took off his coat, shirt and tie, and washed; his movements were still slow, as if he could not really summon up the energy for this, that nothing could refresh him for long. Yet the powerful muscles of his arms and massive shoulders rippled. He was drying himself when there was a tap at the door. A Hopi came in with his two bags and the car key, and a waiter with sandwiches and the drink replaced him before the door closed on him.

Dawlish tipped, thanked, sipped and then ate. He knew that he was hungry, but the food meant little. Finished, he went to the telephone by the side of the bed.

"Can I help you?"
"What time is it, please?"
"It's five after six, sir."
"Call me in two hours' time, please," Dawlish said. "I'll need some waking."
"You'd like a call at eight o'clock, sir?" There was a hint of uncertainty in the operator's voice; the unfamiliar accent and unfamiliar phrasing often caused that note of doubt.
"Please," Dawlish said, "and make sure you wake me."
"I'll do that."
Dawlish rang off, sat on the side of the bed, kicked off his shoes and then lay down, with his head on Felicity's pillow. Even thought of that and the whisper of Felicity's voice could not keep him awake. He hadn't slept, not to say slept, for seventy-two hours. He had driven, night and day, from New York, stopping—and then only briefly—at the places where Felicity had stopped and from where she had written to him. Before that, there had been two tense, almost frightened days in New York, talking to Felicity's friends and hosts; and talking to the police. All had been helpful but none had helped. Before that, he had flown across the Atlantic, after being forced to wait three days for a 'plane—three infuriating days after he had come to the damnable conclusion that Felicity was missing.
At first, he had been simply disappointed at not hearing from her; then had reminded himself that airmail from the West Coast took five days; next had grown restive, cabled the Hollywood family who were to be Felicity's hosts, and received the cabled alarm:

Cable received Felicity has not arrived do not understand why. Checking hospitals.

From that moment fear had flared, fed by the days of silence before his cable; a second from Hollywood had brought a hint of solace; there had been no results from the checking.
It was now the twenty-third day of September, and the date on Felicity's last letter had been the twenty-sixth of August; also a Tuesday.
Dawlish had not written to the guide, who might be called a Ranger, named Bill. He had made as sure as he could that nothing had been amiss with Felicity. She had been alone,

driving a borrowed Ford, carefree, happy, writing to him every second or third day, sometimes only a few sentences, always with: *you'll just have to come, you'll be enthralled*, or with that sentiment.

When he had slept for two hours he could seek out 'Bill'.

CHAPTER II

SHARP INTEREST

THE telephone-bell woke Dawlish when he didn't want to wake. He heard it, cursed it, and it stopped; but soon it started again. He came out of the stupor of sleep, and remembered. He answered the telephone and made himself get up at once, stripped, took a cold shower, and before he dressed, ordered another Scotch-and-soda.

At half past eight he was downstairs, wearing a brown linen suit badly creased from packing, last worn on the French Riviera. Rather than let him walk about with his suit so creased, Felicity would have pressed it with a tiny travelling iron meant for silks and cottons. Everything reminded him of Felicity.

Lights were on, it was chilly because of the altitude, a log fire burned in a huge grate. Dawlish, moving as if he had won new life in two hours, smiled at the room clerk who had signed him in.

"Hallo," he said. "Not busy tonight?"

"It's getting near the end of the season, Mr. Dawlch, it's never so busy just now, but there'll be the usual party on the morning train. I hope you're comfortable in your room."

"It's fine, thanks. My wife was in the same room, four weeks ago."

"Is that so?" The clerk infused a polite interest into the remark. "So you're heading West, after her."

"Yes. Will it be easy to tell me when she booked out?"

The clerk hesitated; and then threw hesitation over. "Why, sure," he said, and busied himself again. "I'd remember Mrs. Dawlch, if I booked her in, but I was sick for three weeks around that time." He took a form from a small pile. "Here it is, Mr. Dawlch—your wife signed in on the twenty-sixth of August and left on the twenty-eighth."

"Two days," said Dawlish. "It isn't enough to look round properly."

"No," agreed the clerk. "You need more than that, especially if you go down to Phantom Ranch."

"Where's that?"

"In the Canyon, sir."

"Can I find out if my wife went down?"

"Sure, we fix the registrations here, Mr. Dawlch, but it will take a little time to check. There's a register down at the ranch, also, but anyone who takes the mule ride doesn't have to sign that."

"Will you find out if my wife went down?"

"Yes, sir, I will."

"Thanks. Where are the guides now, do you know?"

"Mostly at home," said the room clerk, "unless they're out with a client who wants to look around by night, and that doesn't happen so often."

"Can you tell me where I'll find a guide named Bill?" asked Dawlish.

Everything was the same. The burning fire, the couples sitting about, a subdued clatter from the dining-room, voices at the cigar and candy store, the watching, waiting Hopis—everything was the same, except the room clerk. He changed. That showed in his pale grey eyes and sudden stillness. His right hand, resting on the desk, moved; the fingers clutched an invisible ball. He looked into Dawlish's politely smiling face as if seeking things that were not there. When he spoke it was with an effort much greater than the question seemed to demand.

"Bill—Bill who?"

"I don't know," confessed Dawlish, "but he has an English wife."

The room clerk relaxed a little but was still not the man who had shown only polite interest. He was more than interested, he was intent; and the Bill with an English wife was the Bill whose name had brought the change about. There was effort behind his smile and his words, and a hint of wariness.

"I'm afraid you won't find him, Mr. Dawlch." A pause followed, long enough for Dawlish to interrupt; he let the chance go. "He's dead," the room clerk said.

Now it was Dawlish who changed; but outwardly there was only the look of formal regret and a vanishing smile. Inwardly there was cold, clawing terror. It was of the mind and he had known it before, or something close to it. He had learned to repress emotions so that no one else could easily guess they were working on him. At home, he had a reputation as a man of violence; or as one who could be violent if forced to it, and could also be so calm that he could look a stolid fool. Now, he looked foolish.

"Oh. I'm sorry. That's bad."

"How did you come to hear of him, Mr. Dawlch?" The room clerk's left hand had moved beneath the desk; perhaps he thought that Dawlish did not see it move, and guessed that he had pressed a bell, meaning to hold Dawlish here, talking, until his summons was answered.

"Why, my wife mentioned him in a letter."

"Is that so?"

"Remarkable coincidence," Dawlish said, and the smile came again, mechanical and insincere. "Bill's wife came from my home town. And my wife's home town. The town," he added earnestly, "where we live."

"Well, what do you know about that?" the clerk said, without amazement. He glanced to his left; a man was approaching, short, dapper, smooth, with a long face of the kind that would never shave cleanly, thin black hair and a small mouth. "From your home town." He looked openly towards the newcomer now, and greeted, "Mr. Morkel, I'd like you to meet Mr. Dawlch." He still made Dawlish sound exactly like Dawlch.

"I hope you're having a good time here, Mr. Dawlch," said Morkel. His voice was subdued, as if it had been overawed by the Canyon. The rest of him was very much alive, his dark eyes bright and, when he spoke, his lips and face mobile. His arched black eyebrows moved with every word he spoke.

"Only just arrived," Dawlish explained.

"If there's anything I can do for you, just say the word," said Morkel. "I'm the Assistant Manager." He glanced at the room clerk, as if silently requesting an explanation of the summons.

"I will," Dawlish said.

"Mr. Dawlch," said the room clerk, with flat emphasis, "asked about Bill Newton."

The Assistant Manager also changed; not so noticeably as his clerk had done, but change there was. The black eyes became intent, he took a new penetrating interest in Dawlish. First the clerk and now Morkel told Dawlish much—most important, the fact that mystery surrounded the death of the guide named Bill. Terror remained in Dawlish, but in the background; years of training, years of experience, told him how to behave now and even how to control his feelings. His faint, almost foolish smile remained.

"My wife mentioned him." He went through the rigmarole again. "I would have liked the same guide to show me round."

"Yes, I quite understand," Morkel said. "Mr. Dawlish, will you be good enough to spare me a few minutes? In my office?" He no longer said 'Dawlch'.

"Gladly."

"Thank you," said Morkel. "Danny, call Mr. Elliott, will you, and ask him if he can come over right now." He nodded to the room clerk and turned from the desk with Dawlish. He glanced sideways at the big man, who shortened his stride so as to keep in step. The bottom of Dawlish's right ear and the top of Morkel's head, with the pale cranium showing beneath carefully brushed hair, were level. He did not seem like a ready talker to Dawlish, but Dawlish wanted him to talk first.

The office was comfortable, with easy chairs some distance from the desk and telephones. Morkel said: "Won't you sit down, Mr. Dawlish?" and when Dawlish was sitting, long legs stretched out, he added: "What will you have?"

"Nice of you. Is there Scotch-and-soda?"

"Surely." There were bottles in a cabinet and ice in a cold-box; Morkel had small, olive-skinned hands and they moved competently. He poured bourbon on to ice for himself, mixed Dawlish's drink and took it across. "It was a very sad thing about Bill Newton."

"Oh. Yes. Thanks. Your health."

"Health," Morkel echoed, and sipped. His eyes looked bright and black and didn't move, he watched Dawlish with an intensity which only a crisis could justify. "He fell into the Canyon. From the right spot you can see what's left of his body, half a mile down."

Dawlish didn't speak. He couldn't see Bill Newton's body or Felicity's, but could imagine the bones of both, picked clean by vultures, perhaps by coyotes also. He wanted to ask, "Is it alone?" He didn't. He looked as if this were a distressing thing to hear but that the death of a stranger meant little more than the death of a horse or a dog.

"That's dreadful," he said. "And for his wife——"

"It nearly drove her mad," Morkel said soberly.

"I can understand it."

"She's better now but she isn't herself. I guess she won't ever be herself again. We've done everything we can to help her, but——"

"I'm sure you have."

"What *can* help?" Morkel asked. He was shrewd but he wasn't complete master of his feelings and he showed that he was uneasy about Mrs. Newton's distress. "I don't think——" The telephone bell rang. "Oh, excuse me." He went across to the desk eagerly, lifted the receiver but didn't sit down. "Yes?" He listened, interpolating "Yes" now and again but giving Dawlish no clue to what he was hearing. "Yes, thanks, Danny," Morkel said, and made his slip, if it could be called one. "Has Mr. Elliott . . . Oh, that's fine."

He rang off.

"Wilf Elliott is acting chief warden of the Canyon National Park," he said. "No man's done so much to try to help Mrs. Newton." Morkel gave Dawlish the impression that there was a lot to say but wanted Elliott to be here when it was said; the brightness of his eyes seemed to increase. The Deputy Sheriff is sick right now, or I'd have sent for him." He talked nervously, hurriedly. "Bill was a guide, we employed him—that's Fred Harvey, I mean, not the Park. Wilf's a Park employee. National Park." He paused. "Wilf'll be here in a few moments, he was just coming in." He went across to the door and opened it, unable to conceal his eagerness. The door was hardly open when a tall man appeared; yet when Dawlish stood up he proved to be inches taller. "Hi, Wilf," greeted Morkel, "I want you to meet Mr. Dawlish."

Wilf Elliott wore khaki, with a wide leather belt, shapeless trousers and brightly polished brown shoes. He had blue eyes, thin grey hair, a face so brown and dry that it looked withered; he wasn't so much an old man as a man who had been aged and weathered by exposure. His big hand had a nutcracker grip.

"Glad to know you, Mr. Dawlish."

"How are you?" Dawlish murmured.

"Fine, thanks," Elliott turned the English formality into a question, and looked as if he gave the correct answer; he was abundantly fit. He watched Dawlish while Morkel, without asking him what he wanted, poured bourbon on ice. "Thanks, Nicky." He went across to a chair from which he could look at Dawlish, and seemed to wait for Morkel; and his coming added to the tension. "How long are you staying, Mr. Dawlish?"

"I'm trying to make up my mind."

"Wilf," said Morkel explosively, "you remember the Englishwoman who went out with Bill the last morning he was alive?"

"I certainly do." Elliott wasn't surprised by that; obviously Danny had been putting two and two together, and had briefed him. "That is, I remember there was a Mrs. Dawlish, an Englishwoman. Your wife, Mr. Dawlish?"

Neither of them could have guessed at the driving fear in Dawlish.

"Yes." Dawlish put a hand to his pocket for cigarettes; Morkel held out a pack of Pall Mall before he opened the case. "Thanks. You've put it oddly, haven't you? That my wife went out with Bill Newton as a guide, and he fell over the rim of the Canyon soon afterwards." Dawlish's voice was flat, but the words did everything needed, making them ready to talk—so ready that they started at the same time. Morkel stopped first and waved.

"Go ahead, Wilf."

"It just happened that way," Elliott said. "It was the last job Bill did. Your wife said she was interested in the flora of the rim and the Canyon; Bill was mad about the flora, so she hired him for the day. Also, she had been to see him and Marion the night before, they'd become pretty good friends. That was August the twenty-seventh—that's right, isn't it, Nicky?"

"Yes. Mrs. Dawlish left very early next morning." Morkel had it all off by heart. "She paid her bill the night before."

"Habit of ours, when we're due to leave at crack of dawn." Dawlish tried to bring a touch of normality into this, but it wasn't easy because nothing was normal. Both men were holding back a question, holding back thoughts, and he couldn't place those thoughts, knew only that they added to the fear in him. "Do I understand that Bill and my wife spent the whole of the day together?"

"That's so." Elliott went on: "Next morning, after your wife had gone, Bill's body was seen in the Canyon. It wasn't possible to get close to it, but he was lying face uppermost and was recognizable through strong glasses."

"Didn't Bill's wife report him missing?"

"She wasn't home. Bill's sister in Flagstaff was having a baby, Marion went along to spend some time with her. She stayed in Flagstaff overnight. That's the way it is sometimes." Elliott's eyes, as cornflower blue as Dawlish's, didn't shift their gaze; and Morkel watched as intently. The silence became so heavy it was like a blanket, but Dawlish would not lift it.

"Are you sure Bill didn't go home?" Dawlish asked.

"No, sir. But no one saw a light in his house, no neighbours heard him, there was no sign he'd prepared a meal for himself. We aren't *sure* but I'd be surprised if he did."

"I see. Did anyone see my wife leave?"

"A Hopi boy carried her bag down and she started off on Highway 64. She wasn't seen later on Highways 66 or 89 in any direction we can trace. She didn't have breakfast here, but that's not unusual, early morning starters often stop on the road."

Dawlish said nothing.

Elliott was reluctant to go on, but he did, after finishing his drink. "We should like a talk with your wife, Mr. Dawlish. Maybe she could tell us just what happened?"

They didn't know what had happened, but could not have said more clearly that they didn't think that Bill Newton had fallen over the Canyon's rim. Perhaps they had their own theories; certainly this mattered to them, as certainly they were ripe to talk.

Dawlish said slowly: "Maybe she could. But as she isn't here, supposing you tell me what you think happened?" He even forced a smile, while the others exchanged glances and Morkel, as if he couldn't bear the stillness, sprang up, collected their glasses and went to pour more drinks.

CHAPTER III

ONE MAN'S GUESS

ELLIOTT was the man to worry about; the man with ideas, and the man with a purpose. That purpose showed through his eyes and his voice. Slow-speaking, slow-moving, he gave the impression that he had all the time in the world to get what he wanted; and he knew just what that was. Morkel was in this as an outsider; he was almost nervous. Nothing yet thought of was likely to make Elliott nervous in the same way.

"Mr. Dawlish," he said, "will you tell us why you're here? Why you asked for Bill Newton?"

"My wife was here. She wrote a letter and mentioned a guide named Bill and his English wife. I wanted to meet Bill." Blue eyes matched blue; but now Dawlish believed that Elliott was not convinced by the story, sensed even if he did not see some other purpose in the visit; but Dawlish's answer couldn't be easily thrust aside.

"And that's all?" Elliott murmured.

"You still haven't told me what you think happened," Dawlish countered. He was glad that he had taken that catnap; tired as he had been when he had first arrived, he would have been no match for Elliott.

"It's not my job to guess," Elliott said. "But I can tell you that I knew Bill Newton too well to believe he fell over that rim by accident, Mr. Dawlish. I also knew him too well to believe that he jumped over."

The thing that mattered was the thing that Elliott hadn't said: that he thought Newton had been pushed into the Canyon. That didn't need a moment to sink in: Dawlish let it appear that it was taking a long time. He stirred suddenly, put his glass down, and his eyes became angry although there was no anger in him, only the worsening fear.

"Can't you talk straight, Elliott?"

"Mr. Dawlish——" Morkel began.

"Why the hell don't you say what you mean?" Dawlish jumped up; Elliott watched but stayed in his chair. "Then I'll tell you what I think of it."

"I told you it isn't my job to guess."

"Apparently it's your job to invent foul innuendo." Dawlish's eyes blazed with well-simulated wrath. "Any man who thinks that my wife *pushed* Newton over wants his head examined." Elliott didn't answer, Morkel started to speak but Elliott glanced across and stopped him. "That's exactly what you've implied. Who else have you told? Come on, Elliott, who else?" Dawlish went a step closer, towering over the warden.

"All right, we don't have to get excited." Elliott spoke very deliberately. "I haven't suggested that your wife pushed Bill over, Mr. Dawlish, I've just stated that I don't believe he fell or that he would jump, which means that I do believe he was pushed. He wasn't seen again leaving here with your wife in the morning. We've found no one else who saw what happened. We would very much like to have a talk with Mrs. Dawlish. Where is she?"

Dawlish stepped back but remained on his feet; an angry Colossus, but also looking frustrated.

"All this happened a month ago. Why didn't you get round to talking to her before?"

Elliott said simply, "We tried, but we couldn't find her."

It had been bad enough before—to know that Felicity had simply vanished. It was much worse now, because here was evidence that someone had been searching for her; the someone would mean the police; who else would search?

"Who searched?" He had to be sure.

"The police," Elliott answered calmly. He hadn't yet finished trying to size Dawlish up, still watched him very closely. "It was an unofficial search, no one has accused your wife of anything."

"You went damned close to it."

Elliott stood up; Morkel remained in the background, as if he knew that any intervention from him would be useless.

"No one has accused your wife of anything," Elliott repeated calmly, "but the Sheriff of Coconino County made unofficial inquiries in Flagstaff and Williams and along the highways and couldn't find out where your wife went after she left here. She vanished, and her car vanished also. That made us more anxious to talk to her, Mr. Dawlish, and maybe it will help to talk to you. Can you tell us of any reason why she should want to disappear?"

Dawlish said sharply: "She had no reason to want to disappear. She was due to visit friends in Hollywood three days after she left here. She didn't arrive."

Elliott didn't smile, just looked satisfied without being smug because he had the answer to his earlier question.

"And you've come to look for her?"

"I've come to find her."

"That's fine," Elliott said; "that's what we all want. You won't have any objection to talking to the Sheriff about this, will you?"

"The police in New York didn't think it worth worrying about a wife who'd run away from her husband."

Elliott looked as if he were glad of the chance to smile.

"I can see their point of view and understand yours, Mr. Dawlish. I'll telephone Flagstaff, and if the Sheriff is able to come up here, we'll meet later tonight. Meanwhile is there any way I can help you?"

Dawlish pondered, then asked, "Can I see Newton's wife?"

"I don't think she will be able to help."

"I thought she needed help," Dawlish said. "A voice from her home town might be just the thing."

"If you're ready, I'll drive you down," Elliott offered, without comment.

"Let me make my own way," said Dawlish. "Keep it informal. I'd like to walk, anyhow—if it's in easy walking distance."

Morkel came to life again.

"I'll send a boy to show Mr. Dawlish the way, Wilf. He'll be able to find his own way back. Hal won't be out from Flagstaff in less than two hours, that will give plenty of time." He looked relieved to have something that he could do. "Have another Scotch, Mr. Dawlish."

"Not now, thanks."

Elliott shook his head at an unspoken invitation. They left the room together. Dawlish stepped into the dimly-lit lounge with its wooden rocking-chairs and the almost shadowy guests. The dining-room was closed; it was half past nine. Elliott waited while Morkel summoned a boy, gave him instructions, and sent him to the verandah ahead of Dawlish. Elliott shook hands, and said, "I'll see you." Dawlish stepped into the starlit night and into the silence, with the swift-footed Hopi a yard ahead of him.

When Dawlish looked up at the stars, he would think: 'Fel might have stood here, looking up.' At each step, he could imagine that he was in Felicity's footsteps. Now that he was on his own, his expression hidden by the darkness, he had nothing to hide and only his fears to show. It was chilly because of the altitude, but when he shivered it wasn't because of the cold.

Felicity had spent a day with a Canyon guide and disappeared the day afterwards, when the guide's body had been found. No one had said that the remains of a body could lie in the Canyon for a lifetime without being seen by human eyes, but it could. It was small comfort that Elliott didn't appear to believe that Felicity was down there too; but if she were alive, why had she disappeared?

The 'if' hurt like a knife-thrust, but did him good, jolting him out of his mood of despair. He was here to find Felicity, not to take part in some solemn requiem. Felicity *was* life—laughing, gay, part of him; it was sacrilege to allow himself to think that she might be dead.

Now he had to suppress his emotions, deafen himself to her voice, make himself think of the mystery just as a problem. One thing was very different here. At home, he would not have gone far without being recognized. People would say, "*The* Patrick Dawlish?" and if they were uninhibited, add how wonderful it was to meet a detective, a one-time Secret Service ace. He would give the glib answers to questions and put on an act of bland modesty—and everywhere he went he would be watched; people and policemen would wonder what he was up to. No one knew him here; he was just Patrick Dawlish, husband of a lost wife. That suited him. Elliott had wondered why he had been so reticent but would probably assume that he was just being English.

Dawlish smiled; the first smile, even if wry, that he had given naturally for several days. The darkness hid it. The darkness hid nearly everything, but the white tunic of the Hopi showed, two yards ahead now, and Dawlish saw lights at windows and when he looked up at the stars, saw the spiky tops of the fir trees. They walked along a tarred road, his own footsteps rang out but the Indian boy's hardly sounded. A couple walking towards them seemed to be arm-in-arm; their footsteps were quiet, and quickly faded. Someone walked behind Dawlish; he sensed that but did not give it a second thought then.

The Hopi stopped beneath a dim lamp, and pointed towards a street where there were lighted houses on either side.

"It is the fourth house on the right," he said in curiously soft English.

"Thanks."

"You're welcome." The boy turned and was soon lost in the gloom. Dawlish walked towards the fourth house, where there was no light; but if Marion Newton were not in the village, Elliott would have said so; Elliott expected her to be in.

Dawlish passed the third house. All were single-storied and a light outside one showed that it was a frame building with a small verandah at the front; none of them was fenced. He reached the fourth but did not slacken his pace. He reached the fifth and paused, to light a cigarette with slow, deliberate movements. Until then, he had heard what had seemed like an echo of his own footsteps; now, it stopped, as it would if it were an echo. Drawing on the cigarette, he walked on, and the echo came again. He shortened his steps; the echo didn't come.

Someone walked behind him.

Someone had walked behind him from the hotel.

He turned round by another lighted house, but saw no one, although he still heard the footsteps. He walked back towards the house which had now become the fourth on his left, and he was nearly there when he saw a man's head and shoulders against a lighted window. The temptation to let the man know he knew he was there, to catch up with and talk to him, came and went; there might be time for that later. He saw a light at the side of Bill Newton's house as he walked towards the front door. He heard a child crying. After a little searching, he rang the bell. The crying grew louder in spite of footsteps which sounded inside the house. He drew back beneath the porch as the door opened and dim light shone on to his face. He could see a woman but had no idea what she was like, except that she wasn't small, and not as tall as Felicity.

"Do you want something?" The voice was English but with an accent acquired out here; it was sharp, could easily become querulous.

"I'd like to see Mrs. Newton," Dawlish said.

His voice would be a shock in itself; unfamiliar and yet striking a chord which would bring the past suddenly into the present. The woman caught her breath.

"I—I'm Mrs. Newton."

"My name is Dawlish," Dawlish told her. "You met my wife a few weeks ago, I think."

She just said, "Oh." The child inside began to grizzle as if on the verge of sleep. "Oh," repeated Marion Newton, and her breathing quickened before she added, "Won't you come in?" The invitation was mechanical. Dawlish could imagine the storm he had caused in her mind. She stood aside as Dawlish entered, then closed the door, switched on another light, and stood looking at him.

She was quite beautiful, with raven black hair and a pale yet vivid face and blue eyes which looked huge and were glistening, as if shock had brought tears to the surface and she was fighting them away. She was something to see.

"Who—who sent you?" she asked huskily.

"I've just had a talk with Mr. Elliott."

"Oh." She turned and opened the door of a room on the right and switched on a light. It was subdued inside the room—which was long and rather narrow, simply furnished with obvious taste although unfamiliar to the English eye; the furniture was plain, almost severe. Dawlish's eye was caught by a photograph standing on a small table, with a bowl of wild flowers by its side; there was nothing else on the table.

The woman saw him look at it, but didn't speak.

"I'll be back in a moment," she said, and went out so quickly that her feet hardly seemed to touch the floor. Dawlish heard the child whimpering; there was no pause in that, so Marion Newton hadn't gone into the child's room. Dawlish turned to the window. The light in here was enough to show Dawlish against the glass but that didn't deter him. He stood by the side, a hand against the big single window, trying to see out; he fancied that he saw a man in the road, standing and watching, but couldn't be sure.

Marion came back; he thought that she had run a comb through her glossy hair, but she hadn't made up; she hardly needed make-up, her beauty was so vivid. He had an impression of tautness, of curiously restrained vitality. She looked at him intently, and he guessed that whatever she said wouldn't be anything he might have expected.

"At least *you'll* believe me," she said, and there was sharp defiance in her voice. "They don't—oh, they say they do, but they don't. I don't care what he might have done before, he wouldn't have done what they think. Not now. He might have done years ago, but not now. It was that damned Canyon. He loved it and I hated it, I knew it would get him, I *knew*."

"Did you?" asked Dawlish gently.

"Sometimes I think it was all he really cared for, and Judy and I——" Her voice went husky, she stopped and turned away. In the line of her face, the shape and movement of her body, there was rare beauty; and a simple frock of lemon-coloured linen emphasized that beauty of body. She turned back to face him; it was like looking at tragedy. "Oh, I'm sorry," she said huskily. "I hardly know what I'm saying or thinking these days, it's—it's hell."

"It must be."

"And he liked her. Sometimes he made me mad, making fun of the English, but he liked Mrs. Dawlish, he was going to enjoy showing her around. I don't care what Elliott or any of the others think, he didn't——"

She broke off again; the words were stemmed, like a torrent coming unexpectedly against the dam—but they would soon flood over it.

"What do they say?" prompted Dawlish.

"They don't say it to *me*, but I know what they're thinking, I can tell from the way they look at me, from the pity in their eyes. They think . . ." She paused again, and Dawlish held his breath, not knowing exactly what was coming but convinced it would hurt. Then she burst out: "They think he made love to her, there was a struggle, she pushed him over!"

The woman stopped, aghast, but Dawlish's wooden expression did nothing to discourage her.

"Or else they both fell over, struggling. I don't believe it, I won't, I can't! I think she slipped over the rim and he tried to save her—they're both down there."

There was no doubt that she believed it, little that she was sure in her heart that 'they' were right despite her denials, that Bill Newton had 'made love' and been resisted, thrust away and sent to his death.

That was a thing Elliott probably believed but hadn't said.

The woman turned and looked at the photograph.

CHAPTER IV

THE SHERIFF

To THE woman, the dead man would seem alive inside that frame. In it, Bill Newton looked a man to whom life meant everything. Handsome became just a hackneyed word. In the black and white, vitality showed; the eyes laughed and beckoned as if nothing could ever dim them. His wife probably heard his voice, day and night, as Dawlish so often heard Felicity's. And in a nearby room there was a child to remind her of all that she had lost.

She turned her head to look at Dawlish, and even with that slight movement, the grace showed; she would quicken the blood of most men, as her husband had quickened the heartbeats of women. She had told him much more than the actual words that she had used. Newton had been a man with a roving eye, a gay Lothario, whose beckoning gaze could bring women to him readily, eagerly; and this girl knew that, but believed he no longer beckoned others. Shock, loss and grief had unsteadied her mind, so that she could say one thing and mean another; contradict herself sentence by sentence. Dawlish knew now what Morkel had meant about the difficulty of helping her. Tragedy had come near to driving her mad; and the knowledge that those who knew her husband had their own ideas about what had happened, that they thought Bill had tried to win a woman once too often, added to the torment.

If she could get that dread out of her mind, she might win a form of calmness.

"So they think they struggled and fell over the rim, and you believe my wife slipped and he went over, trying to save her." Dawlish said. He looked away from the photograph and took out cigarettes, quite casually. She felt for one, watching him all the time. He flicked his lighter and shook his head. "Nonsense," he added, and held the flame towards her.

She didn't move to light the cigarette.

"What do you mean?"

"It just didn't happen their way or yours." He let the flame go out. "I know it didn't."

Her eyes blazed, as if with new life, and her voice was taut. "How could you know?"

He smiled easily; there was no reason why Marion should guess that he was lying, or how the lie hurt.

"I heard from her afterwards. If anything like that had happened, she would have mentioned it. Oh, she wouldn't have gone into detail, just said something about the ardour of some Americans!" He actually managed to laugh. "Even if I hadn't heard, I would still say that it didn't happen that way—not with Felicity. She could cool the ardour of the most eager with that down-the-nose look of hers."

"I—see," said Marion Newton. She moved back from him, one hand behind her, groping for a chair. He didn't help, just waited for her to sit down; the cigarette was still between her fingers. He lit his own. She didn't turn her gaze away for a moment, and her eyes burned, as if hope were coming back—and with hope would come the first healing. "She—she wrote *after* she left here?"

"Just a card. Dated August the twenty-eighth. All this happened the day before. She was very cheerful and said she'd had a wonderful time—seen seventy-eight varieties of wild flowers and a dozen birds she'd never seen before. All went well that day, Marion, whatever went wrong happened after she'd left Bill."

"Oh," said Marion, and looked down at her cigarette, as if surprised to find it there. She put it to her lips and Dawlish lit it for her. "Thank you. You—you'll never know what a relief that is."

"Pity I didn't come before," Dawlish said.

"Why *have* you come?"

"I'm to join her in Hollywood."

"But—but I understand that the police can't find her!"

"She's touring. They'll catch up. She probably hasn't the faintest idea about what's happened." He didn't want to overdo it, if he emphasized it too much he might cause doubt. For him it was like holding an open knife in his hand, with the blade cutting into his palm. "People talk and gossip as much here as at home, then, and jump to wild conclusions. Would you rather be back home?"

That switched her thoughts.

"Sometimes I think I would. I don't know. I've grown used to it here, and—everyone's been so kind. They *are* kind. But I've known what they've been thinking, although they tried to hide it from me. Bill's sister wants me to go and live with them for a while—in Flagstaff. It's been so difficult to try to decide what to do. Are you—are you going to stay here long?"

"I'm afraid not."

"You'll tell the others about hearing from your wife, won't you?"

"I'll tell Elliott."

"That will be enough," Marion said. "He's been—he's been impossibly good. Everyone has. Sometimes I feel more at home here than I ever did in England." She gave a swift apologetic smile. "Is that disloyal?"

"Lord, no!" exclaimed Dawlish, and laughed. "Home is where you make it. I came out here full of prejudice about loud-mouthed Yanks, and I haven't yet met one I haven't liked. Elliott's typical, if there is a type." He still talked casually, and she was eager to listen.

After a few minutes she jumped up.

"What am I thinking about? I haven't offered you a drink." In the flush of relief she was almost happy. That would fade, but torment wouldn't come so close again, unless something happened to tell her that Dawlish had lied. She hadn't any Scotch; he drank bourbon and chased it with ice-cold water.

She took him in to see Judy, a red-cheeked two-year-old, fast asleep now, clutching a woolly doll. She showed him photographs of Bill's sister and her husband, their two children, their frame house, holiday snaps of Bill, a dozen pictures of Judy. It was difficult for Dawlish to say that he must go, and it was nearly twelve o'clock when he left. The woman stood on the porch with the light behind her, a hand raised. She was still there when he reached the corner.

So was the man.

It was quite dark, except for the stars; no lights were on along the road, and there was silence—except for Dawlish's footsteps and the echo that was not an echo. He found his way back without difficulty, and there was light at the foot of the steps leading to the hotel and at the hotel itself. Several people still sat out on the verandah. Dawlish went halfway up the steps, stopped, and went down again. A man was coming towards the hotel; *the* man? Dawlish kept in the shadows. The man walked slowly now; before, he had walked quickly. He passed beneath a light, without glancing towards Dawlish or showing any sign that he knew Dawlish was there. He wore a ten-gallon hat, a dark shirt and belted pants. He passed the steps without turning up to the hotel. Dawlish followed him, but he didn't look round. He reached the rim of the Canyon; the night hid the mountain ranges of that world below their feet. There was nothing to see. The man stood looking into the darkness, then turned right. Dawlish followed, ten yards behind him, able to see the silhouette of head and shoulders and big hat against the sky. The other's footsteps were soft, like those of the man who had followed Dawlish, but there was no certainty that it was the same man.

Dawlish kept to the side of the path away from the rim. He made no sound. If the other turned and looked, he would see only blackness.

Another man approached, from the opposite direction, walking quickly. Both men slowed down and Dawlish stood still. A whispered voice came:

"Trig?"

"Yeah."

"How did you make out?"

The man named Trig said, "He went to Newton's house."

"So he did," said the other.

Dawlish heard not only their voices but the dynamo he called a heart pounding within him. He fought against it, fearful that it would deafen him. His hands were clenched at his sides and his chin thrust out; above all things he wanted to rush forward; taken by surprise, they would have little chance against a tempest.

He kept rigid.

Trig waited for the other to speak.

"He talked with Morkel and Elliott," the man said slowly.

"What's news?" That was almost a sneer.

"Keep watching him," the second man said.

"No one's told me to stop."

The second man turned on his heel; Dawlish heard rather than saw the movement. "See you," he said, and went off, walking very quickly. Dawlish didn't move. Trig turned slowly, walked past Dawlish and appeared to see nothing, stopped a few yards farther on and lit a cigar. Dawlish could see only the outline of his hat and head and shoulders, not his face. The man dropped the match and trod it out, then walked towards the hotel, went up the steps and took a seat in a dark corner. He hadn't shown his face. Dawlish turned; there would be another way into the hotel, although he hadn't yet found it.

He did, without difficulty. Danny the room clerk was on duty, and went out of his way to beam a welcome. Dawlish smiled back, didn't pause, but went on to the verandah, visible against the light.

From here, Dawlish could see the shadowy figure of Trig. He wanted Trig in a good light, but couldn't think how to fix that. Trig, by turning his head, could see all he wanted to. Trig had a voice which Dawlish wouldn't easily forget, but seeing was much more important than hearing. He went back into the hotel, hurrying, and the room clerk called:

"Mr Dawlish!"

"Later." Dawlish waved and went along the corridor to the side entrance, out and across the road outside the hotel towards the car park, moving at speed all the time, making little sound. The convertible stood waiting, he'd been given back the keys. He climbed in, started the engine and swung out of the car park; seconds might count. He followed the white arrows on the road until the headlights shone on to the hotel, then on to the verandah—then on to Trig.

It was the man. He sat in the once dark corner, face shown up in sharp relief by the baleful light. It was a long face, with a long, pointed jaw, with a small nose. Trig turned his face away to avoid the glare, but his profile was as sharp as an etching. He couldn't see the driver of the car which passed. Dawlish quickened his speed as he went by the hotel, turned away from the car park towards the station, and stopped the car in a recess on the side of the road. He got out. Hurrying had made him hot, and a soft wind struck cold. He went in by the side entrance without going up the verandah steps, and found the room clerk and Morkel talking, as if anxiously, one on each side of the desk.

"Want me?" he asked mildly.

Morkel swung round.

"Why, there he is," said the room clerk foolishly.

Morkel's smile showed deep relief; could he have had a wild thought that Dawlish had been running away?

"We've been looking for you, Mr. Dawlish."

"Is everyone here?"

"Yes, and waiting."

"That couldn't be better," Dawlish said. "The quicker it's over, the quicker I can get to bed." He fell into step with Morkel and they were soon in the office. Tobacco smoke filled the large, bright room, coming from one pipe—Elliott's—and the cigar of a thin man—one so thin that he didn't look real. He had a hatchet face, it was easy to imagine a touch of Indian blood. He sat in one of the big chairs, a drink by his side, with Elliott opposite him; both gave the impression that they hadn't a care in the world or the slightest need to hurry, now or ever.

They stood up.

"Hal, this is Mr. Dawlish," Elliott said. "This is Hal Morgan, Sheriff of Coconino County, Mr. Dawlish."

Morgan's hand was bony but powerful. He drawled, "I'm happy to meet you," and smiled. The smile was as lazy as the man looked; but for the brightness of small grey eyes he would have seemed incapable of effort. His drawl was more pronounced than Elliott's, so marked that to Dawlish it seemed affected. "Yes, I'm surely happy to meet you, Mr. Dawlish," he repeated. "I've been hearing about you. Wilf Elliott says you won't object if I ask you a few questions." His smile suggested that it had been ridiculous to think that Dawlish would object; a reassuring man.

"None at all," Dawlish said, "but don't make it too many. I've had two hours' sleep in three days."

He wanted to be away, to get his mind clear for thinking. Trig was something to think about; so was the smaller man who had walked up sharply and talked to him and then hurried off. He might like the look of the Sheriff, but the police had been trying to find Felicity for a long time, and they'd failed. In searching for her, he wanted no handicaps; there had never been a job more truly his, and his alone.

"We need not take long," Morgan said, and his drawl made the sentence lengthy; he could become wearisome. "The first question I'll be glad if you'll answer, Mr. Dawlish is just this." He paused, and glanced at his cigar. Morkel from one side and Elliott from the other watched Dawlish, not the Sheriff. "Did your wife have any special reason for coming to the Canyon?" Morgan asked. "Did she know Bill Newton before she arrived here?"

CHAPTER V

THE WISDOM OF SHERIFF MORGAN

FIRST there had been Elliott, insisting that Newton had been pushed, hinting, even though he denied it, that Felicity had done the pushing. Now here was Sheriff Morgan, showing that he considered even if he did not suspect possibilities which in themselves were absurd. The question mattered to him; was the key question.

Dawlish said, "No."

"You sure about that?" Morgan hitched himself up more comfortably in his chair.

"I'm quite sure. There is no possibility of it."

"Can you be sure of that?" Morgan wasn't accusing, just trying to reassure himself, because the question had mattered and the answer was disappointing; and the manner of it made the answer seem simple truth. "Can you be so sure?"

Dawlish said briefly, "Yes."

"Maybe I'm just an old man with too little to do and too much time for thinking," Morgan said, and his smile was the smile of a wizened cherub, "but this is the way I've been wondering, Mr. Dawlish. You and your wife come from the same home town as Mrs. Newton."

"Yes."

"Maybe you and your wife knew Mrs. Newton before she was married, and——"

"We didn't."

Morgan looked down at his cigar, considered, and then his bright little eyes shone into Dawlish's.

"This township of Haslemere in England, Mr. Dawlish, is it of any considerable size?"

Dawlish began to smile.

"It's a small town by our standards, with about six or seven thousand people," he said. "My wife and I have lived on the outskirts for eight years. We know a hundred people fairly well and perhaps another two hundred by sight. It is just possible that when my wife saw Marion Newton she recognized her as someone she had seen before, but that isn't what you're after, is it? You want to know if she came here to see Marion."

"That's what I want to know."

"Why should you think she had?"

"I didn't get that far," temporized Morgan, "I just got round to wondering." He stopped. No one else spoke. Morkel came across with a Scotch-and-soda and put it by Dawlish's side. The "thanks" and "you're welcome" were subdued. Morgan was trying to get inside Dawlish's mind; perhaps he knew more or suspected more than he had yet said. It could be because of Bill Newton's reputation; it could be about something else, something Dawlish had no reason to suspect. He had reason to be uneasy, to wonder where this probing was getting, what was in the Sheriff's deep mind.

"I've just come from Marion Newton," Dawlish said.

Morgan nodded.

"She will probably be better from now on." Dawlish picked up his drink. "She had some idea that everyone here, including Mr. Elliott, thought that her Bill had made passionate love to my wife and been repulsed—going over the rim in the process. She didn't agree, and now she knows she was right." He drank.

Morkel moved forward, Elliott raised a hand, the Sheriff didn't move a muscle except at his lips when he said:

"What put the idea out of her mind, Mr. Dawlish?"

"I told her that I'd heard from my wife after she left here and that if there had been anything unpleasant I would have heard of it. Do you agree with me that a lie can sometimes have a virtue, Sheriff?"

Morgan began to smile, without opening his lips.

"Did she believe you?" Elliott asked, abruptly.

"I think I convinced her."

"It could be you've given her what she needed," conceded Morgan, and there was little doubt that he approved. "If it *was* a lie, Mr. Dawlish." He still smiled, a droll and leathery smile.

"The last letter I had from my wife was written from here on the evening of August twenty-sixth." The truth had to be told here. "Can we go on from that? How many other people thought that Newton was unpleasant, my wife resisted, Newton fell over, and my wife ran away?" He took out cigarettes. "I won't do violence, Sheriff!"

Morkel said abruptly: "We *all* thought that."

He spoke out of turn; Morgan showed that he thought so with a swift glance which would probably subdue the Assistant

Manager until the end of the interview. Dawlish lit his cigarette. Elliott kept quiet, although there was now no need.

"It was in some people's minds," Morgan agreed, "I wouldn't say in everybody's. No, sir. Bill was a fine fellow but he had his weaknesses and a nice-looking woman was one of them. Mr. Dawlish, Bill Newton was stationed at this township of Haslemere for most of two years. That's how he came to meet his wife. You and your wife would give hospitality to our boys, I guess?"

"Not to Bill. We didn't see Bill. But if we'd known Bill, if he and my wife had known each other, perhaps had an *affaire* in England, it would explain why she came and went out for the day with Bill."

Morgan grinned. "You don't have to be told much, Mr. Dawlish."

"You have to be told this," Dawlish said quietly. "That isn't the way it happened. They were complete strangers. I don't believe that Felicity would let any hot-headed Don Juan get so far as a struggle. I don't think she had anything to do with Bill's death. How far does that take us, Sheriff?"

After a long while, Morgan said: "Maybe this far. Someone else pushed Bill over."

"Or he fell."

Morgan looked humorously at Elliott.

"You aren't so convincing, Wilf," he said. "Okay, Mr. Dawlish, we'll allow that it could have happened either way."

"You could get the body up and find out if he were really killed by the fall?" Dawlish said.

Morgan shook his head slowly.

"Not down beneath the Big Rock, friend. If a man falls, he stays there. We've had men die searching for lost wanderers. If a child falls, he stays. In parts of the Canyon we can search, but in others there isn't a chance for anyone. I've seen men cut to ribbons by the catsclaw and the mesquite; driven mad by the sun and the desolation. No, sir. Bill Newton's bones are there to stay. Anyone who falls over near the Big Rock is there to stay. Eh, Wilf?"

Elliott nodded, once.

"So where do we go next?" Morgan asked. "According to your thinking, your wife vanished from here on August twenty-eighth, but not because of Bill's death."

"Not because of her share in Bill's death," Dawlish amended.

Until then, perhaps because of the stimulus of being followed by and following Trig, and the stimulus of the challenge in Morgan's manner, it had been possible to be detached, to see it as a problem. Suddenly it stopped being just that. It was a matter of life and death—Felicity's life and death. It brought back the surging tumult of anxiety and fear.

Dawlish covered the swift change with a wooden expression and doubted if any of the others guessed at it; but no harm would come if they did guess.

"You could tell us what you mean, Mr. Dawlish," Morgan invited.

Dawlish said harshly: "I mean that my wife came out here on a sight-seeing trip, that she disappeared, that she might be dead. I mean that Bill Newton might have been pushed over the Canyon on the morning when she left, not the night before—and that she might have seen it." He stood up slowly. "And if she saw it, then someone would have a good reason to want her dead."

His voice put tension into the atmosphere, he looked savage, deadly. When he went on it was almost as slowly as Morgan, but there was none of Morgan's drawl.

"And I'm going to find out what's happened to her, Sheriff. You've had four weeks, and you haven't got very far."

Morgan said mildly: "Not far enough. I guess no one regrets that more than I do. Sit down, Mr. Dawlish." He waited. Dawlish could have been obstinate but saw no purpose in it. He dropped into a chair. Morkel came and collected his glass, and Elliott interposed:

"The Sheriff's done all it was possible to do."

Dawlish grunted; the grunt said all that he thought of Morgan's efforts, but Morgan wasn't affronted. He sat holding his dead cigar and looking as if he had all the time in the world and did not know the meaning of urgency.

"See it this way," he suggested. "Bill's fall could have been an accident. There's no way of being sure. I could ask neighbouring counties for news of your wife but I couldn't go further than that, and there was no news. Men have fallen over the Canyon's rim before, and never been seen—Bill Newton was seen, so that we soon knew what had happened to him. Eh, Wilf? The most likely explanation was this quarrel and struggle. We don't know of anyone around here with a good reason for pushing Bill over." His smile screwed up his eyes and showed up a thousand crowsfeet. "Since he came home, Bill's behaviour has been so good most of us couldn't believe it. He could have had a relapse. Eh, Wilf?"

Elliott nodded.

"You see," Morgan said.

"So you looked for a motive, thought you had one, thought my wife had run away, but there was no evidence against her," Dawlish said. "Certainly there was nothing big enough to make you take it to the Federal authorities who could inquire in England. Is that it?"

"You don't need telling anything twice," Morgan said. "There are some things you don't seem to need telling at all, Mr. Dawlish."

Dawlish went on, "And you haven't looked for any other motive."

"I'd rather you said that we haven't found one," Morgan corrected smoothly. "We haven't even been able to think one up. You see this from a different angle, maybe it's the right angle—it's one no person could get unless they knew your wife as you know her. Now we took one view that seemed the obvious one, and you take one that doesn't seem so obvious—to us." Morgan put his cigar to his lips and lit it; he had been wanting to do that all the time. He clamped it firmly between his teeth and it hardly moved as he spoke; his lips moved slightly. "That Bill was pushed over, your wife saw it, and she had to be silenced." His drawl and his quietness gave that an unbearable vividness. "Is that *all* guesswork, Mr. Dawlish?"

"Call it what you like."

"If we had some reason for thinking it might be true . . ." Morgan didn't finish.

This was Dawlish's job, and his alone. Wasn't it? From the moment he had arrived here, he had assumed that and believed it. He hadn't reckoned on finding a policeman with an open mind. Now he started to think again. In England, he would know all the ropes; police methods, the habits, even the turn of mind of the people with whom he would have to deal. He had none of those advantages here. He talked the same language but in a way which made him conspicuous. He did not know the country; Elliott and the Sheriff would know every trail, every glade. Was he right in thinking that the others couldn't help? What mattered, except finding Felicity? If Morgan found her, if one of the Hopi boys found her, life would begin again.

He said abruptly, "Do you know a man named Trig?"

It meant nothing to Morgan, who shook his head and glanced at Elliott.

"No," said Elliott. "Trig?"

"One 'g' or two, I don't know," Dawlish said. "I——"

"*Trig?*" exclaimed Morkel. He moved forward; Dawlish thought that the others had also almost forgotten that he was present. "I know a Trig Clay, he's staying in one of the huts right now. Comes here most years, sometimes two or three times. What's this about Trig?" His black eyes were bright with excitement, partly at being brought back into the centre of things.

Dawlish said, "Elliott——"

Elliott said, "I've placed him, now." He looked as if he didn't know whether this were worth excitement or not. "He just loafs around. Bill and he used to get along."

"What does he look like?" Dawlish asked. "Long chin, small nose——"

"That's Clay!" exclaimed Morkel.

Dawlish said, "Elliott, did you have anyone follow me from the hotel tonight?"

"I did not."

"Morkel?"

"No, sir."

"I was followed," Dawlish said flatly. "You can assume that it was Trig. Just before I came back, I followed him for a change. He met another man, who wasn't named. The other man knew about our talk here earlier, told Trig to keep on watching. Can you think of any reason why Trig should do that? Why anyone should want him to?"

For the first time, the room seemed to burn with the excitement of the other men; even Morgan's. And as it burned, Dawlish found doubts thundering into his mind—doubts about telling them, doubts about letting any of this out of his own hands. Morkel brought the final clap of thunder.

"Why don't we go see Trig right now?" he demanded.

CHAPTER VI

MORNING RUN

THERE were a thousand reasons why they should want to see Trig. There was no reason in the world why they should agree with Dawlish—that if anyone saw Trig, it must be he. They had a mystery to solve and what might be a murder to investigate, and it stopped there. So Clay could be questioned now. Dawlish had a wife to find. He had to fight against his own impulses, work with judgment which might be warped; he didn't want to question Clay yet; saw that as a fatal step.

Morkel was almost hopping in his eagerness to go and talk to Trig Clay.

If he argued now, Dawlish knew they would wonder why, and find it easy to ignore him; if they did that, there would be nothing he could do about it.

"We could all go," Morkel said eagerly.

"Sure, we could do that," agreed Morgan, taking his cigar from his lips. "What would we say to him?"

Dawlish began to breathe more easily.

"We want to know why he followed Dawlish, don't we? Why *should* he follow Dawlish, why should he be interested in him?"

"What makes you think Trig would tell us?" asked Morgan. "How clearly did you see him, Mr. Dawlish?"

"At first, in the darkness. So I went for my car and put him under the headlights. I'll recognize Trig again." He didn't add a cautious note, preferred to leave this to Morgan; Morgan had the kind of mind it would be easy to get along with.

"So Dawlish can identify him." Morkel could see nothing else to stop them from going for Trig.

"Which would make it one man's word against another's. Trig would deny it. It would also tell Trig—Clay, did you say?"

"That's right, Trig Clay."

"It would also tell Clay that he had been observed," went on Morgan, "and if they have good reason to follow Dawlish, then maybe someone whom Dawlish doesn't know would take over that job. Would you like to go and see Clay right now, Dawlish?"

Dawlish shook his head.

"He would be easy to watch," Elliott put in. "I could have one of my park-rangers—well, I guess *all* of my boys—keeping a look-out for him. It would be no trouble at all."

"It would be so easy," Morgan conceded. "And just as easy for one of the rangers to ask Clay what it's all about." He wrinkled his eyes at Dawlish. "I guess you and me are seeing this the same way, Mr. Dawlish."

Dawlish found that he could grin. "There are some things that I don't have to tell you at all," he said.

Morgan chuckled, Elliott grinned, only Morkel found it difficult to see what amused them. He thought they were wrong, but in this Morgan's word counted most. Morgan hadn't stirred from his chair, and still looked as if nothing could be urgent; looked, also, as if he were prepared to spend the rest of the night in that big chair. He proved himself a diplomat, held out his empty glass to Morkel, and said thoughtfully:

"You could be more right than you are, Nicky, I guess we ought to consider that. I don't think we need worry about Clay taking a powder tonight, and if we change our minds we can talk to him in the morning.

"It's your decision, I guess." Morkel took the glass.

"When we make one it has to be right," Morgan said. "And there are plenty of things to consider." That was for Morkel's benefit, too. "Are you aware of what you've done for us, Mr. Dawlish? You've suggested that Bill Newton was murdered and if you haven't lied—and I confess I can't see any reason why you should—you've made it clear that someone is mighty interested in you. Why should that be? Because they realize you've come to look for your wife, and to find out what happened to her? They surely know we've been looking and haven't found her, so they're watching you to make sure you don't have more luck." He glanced at Elliott. "Am I making sense, Wilf?"

"I imagine they believe we've given up, but they won't expect Dawlish to give up so easily. Also, they don't know what his wife wrote to Dawlish. They aren't troubled by us, Hal, but they could be troubled by Dawlish."

Morgan grinned again.

"Meaning by 'us' they haven't been troubled by me. That's so." He sat up for the first time, took his refilled glass from Morkel, sipped, and said more quickly than he had spoken before: "Can you give me one reason you haven't mentioned why Clay or anyone should be interested in you, Mr. Dawlish?"

"No."

Elliott said: "Why don't we wait and see what happens tomorrow? See if the man Clay follows Mr. Dawlish again. We can have one or two of the boys keep a close watch on Dawlish, to see nothing happens to him."

Morgan said: "Wilf hasn't the same high opinion of you as I have, Mr. Dawlish, he doesn't think you can look after yourself! Will you take that risk?"

"If I knew it were deadly, I'd still take it," Dawlish said. "I don't see it as a risk yet. Just one question." He looked at them each in turn. "If Trig Clay *doesn't* know what happened to my wife, why should he be interested in me?"

No one answered.

Dawlish stood up. "He may still be on the verandah. Why not say good night out there, Sheriff? You can tell me how sorry you are you can't help me." He kept a straight face.

Morgan's was quite blank, too.

"Sure, we'll do that. You needn't come out, Nicky. You'll be on your way, Wilf, won't you?" He finished his drink. "Thanks for the hospitality, Nicky."

"Forget it," Morkel said.

Only one light, in the doorway, shone on to the verandah. It showed no one. Dawlish went to the head of the steps, the other two by his side. Trig Clay wasn't sitting in his shadowy seat; the verandah and the grounds around it seemed deserted. Voices travelled clearly on the still air.

"I can only say I'm mighty sorry," Morgan said, "if I could help you I'd be right glad to, Mr. Dawlish. But Mrs. Dawlish certainly left here."

Dawlish said stiffly: "You've been very good."

"If there's a thing we can do to help, just say the word." Elliott meant that, it wasn't only for the sake of anyone who might be listening.

"Thanks."

"Will you stick around for long?" asked Morgan.

"She was heading for Hollywood," Dawlish said. "I'll do the same. I may——" He broke off. "I may stay for a day or two. Good night." He shook hands with them both, and turned and hurried back into the hotel.

He didn't go upstairs, but to the side entrance, and the two men were still walking on the roadway outside the hotel when he reached it a hundred yards behind them.

The silhouette of a ten-gallon hat showed against the sky, halfway between. Trig Clay had been listening in the bushes near the entrance. He had probably been convinced that Dawlish was as hopeless as he sounded. He waited until the two men's footsteps had faded, then followed, making little sound. The easiest thing in the world would have been to follow him. Dawlish went as far as the verandah steps, then turned into the hotel.

Upstairs, he got into the bed where Felicity had slept, and there was hope as well as fear in him.

• • • • •

Dawlish had breakfast at a table overlooking the Canyon. with the morning sun burning down into it and the colours pale. He hadn't seen Morkel, but the dining-room staff and a different room clerk had treated him as a celebrity. It was half past nine when he finished and went out, hatless, massive, slow-moving, and with a set face. There were dozens of people whom he hadn't seen about the night before; off the train which room clerk Danny had told him would be in that morning. Two or three men, who had something of the look of Elliott, were about. A small touring bus stood outside the front door of the hotel, passengers already in it, a man with a face not unlike Bill Newton's, but less handsome, was calling to others who were hurrying from the hotel. Dozens of people were at the nearest point of the Canyon's rim: the place seemed alive.

Trig Clay wasn't in sight.

Dawlish walked along the path, with its view-points into the Canyon, stopping to look, finding the awesome sight forcing thought out of his mind. It was as if he were gazing into infinity. He turned away but the Canyon seemed to draw his gaze; yet he could not gaze upon it too long at a time.

It dulled his senses. He had to force himself to remember that he should find out if anyone else were interested in him; if anyone else had replaced Trig Clay. He noticed no one following; but he could be watching from a distance, there would be many vantage points.

He walked for twenty minutes, always farther from the

hotel. The path led away from the rim, there were rocks and stunted trees and bushes on either side. Between the bushes he caught an occasional glimpse of the Canyon, and it had the same beckoning influence; like Bill Newton's eyes.

Where was Big Rock, where Bill Newton's skeleton lay, beneath the mountain-tops and the skies?

No one was behind Dawlish now; as far as he knew, no one was within sight. But the rocks and the trees might hide Trig Clay or the man whom Clay had met the night before. Silence laid a haunting hand upon the earth, as if it were coming out of the Canyon and touched the rim itself; but the birds were in song, untouched, without awe. Dawlish had them and the humming insects for company, but not one human.

There was Felicity's voice.

There was Elliott's conviction that Newton had been pushed over, and Sheriff Morgan's drawling shrewdness and understanding eyes. Was it wrong to think that Morgan had been ready, almost eager to believe that there was more in the death of the ranger than had appeared? That was an idea, no more; and the very atmosphere and sense of loss gave credence to ideas which, at other times and in other places, could easily be scoffed at. It was easy now to scoff at his own fears for himself; to think that he had imagined Trig Clay and the hurrying man and the silhouette of the broad-brimmed hat against the starlit sky. If they had watched him then, why didn't they watch now? He was so utterly alone.

He turned a corner.

A man said, "Okay, Dawlish, that's far enough."

It wasn't Clay's voice; it wasn't the voice of the man who had spoken to Clay. No one was in sight. Dawlish stopped, his breathing suddenly soft, his mind stung to sudden alertness; but although he looked at every gap in the trees, he saw no one.

"Come this way," the man said. "Step off the path."

The voice came from the land between the path and the Canyon's rim, a quiet, confident voice, that of a man who knew exactly what he was doing and would do it well. It was an American voice.

Dawlish stood still.

"Walk," another man said.

This was closer and behind Dawlish. He looked behind him and saw no one. There was just the silence, broken by the laconic voices which might have come out of the air. He did not move, and kept his hands in sight, although there was a gun in his hip pocket, its shape hidden by the bulk of his coat. The stillness seemed to envelop Dawlish and the sun burned on his fair head.

"Just walk," the second voice repeated. "Go towards that big rock."

Was that *the* Big Rock? It was twenty feet high, as far round at the base.

Dawlish stared into the scrub and tree-clad patch and for the first time saw the man—or what he thought was a man's legs, where the scrub was thin. He judged the position, then turned slowly and took two steps forward, as if about to obey. The dynamo inside him hammered. On the second step, he spun on his right foot and lunged forward between a gap in the trees and towards the man he had seen. The man *was* there; he appeared for a split second before darting out of sight, behind a rock.

"Keep still!"

He wasn't within a hand's reach, but the rock which covered him also covered Dawlish. Dawlish kept his hand away from his pocket.

"I don't play that way," he said, "I like to see who I'm talking to."

"Just turn round and walk towards that big rock," the man said. He hadn't the confidence of the first speaker, and Dawlish's rush had shaken him. But he was protected and he probably carried a gun.

Dawlish growled, "To hell with you." He turned back to the path, and as he touched it, the first man spoke again.

"This way, Dawlish, and cut out the funny stuff."

Dawlish stared at the trees, saw no one, but placed the spot where he thought the man was; ten yards away or more, too far for him to reach in a surprise attack. He turned and faced the hotel, half an hour's walk away. Except for the birds and the insects there was no other sound. He began to walk towards the hotel, without haste. He neared a curve in the gravel path.

"Don't come any farther."

This time a third voice, ahead of him; so they were all round him. No one had seemed to follow, but three had, and there might be more. He took another step forward—and stopped abruptly. A lightning flash appeared before his eyes, the blade of a knife caught in the sun. It flashed past him, inches away from his head, and he heard it strike a rock and clatter to the ground.

"Next time it will cut you open," said the man in front. "Turn round, and go towards the Big Rock."

Not far off, a car engine sounded, grew louder, and then faded slowly into the silence; so there was a road near here. When the silence fell again, it seemed more intense, laden with the menace of the unseen men. Dawlish turned again, slowly, as if with fear and reluctance. The Big Rock stood out among the others, taller than most of the trees. He took a step towards it, and the man behind him said:

"You can go faster than that."

He went a little faster. He hadn't moved to take his gun, hoping that the others would assume that he didn't carry one. He stepped off the path. His breathing was quick and shallow, his movements nervous, fast, because he seemed to be nearer a source of the truth than he had been, or had expected to be so soon.

He reached the rock.

Now the voices were all behind him, and the man who had spoken first said:

"Go round to the other side."

Dawlish looked about him, saw no one, felt as if the voices were coming out of nowhere, was touched by a sense of unreality. He made himself go forward, reached the side of the rock and stopped: and held his breath.

The earth fell away. A few feet ahead was a sheer drop into the Canyon.

CHAPTER VII

THE LEDGE

DAWLISH stood motionless.

He could not go forward, or the Canyon would swallow him up. To the right and left and behind him, there would be the men; and one could throw a knife. If he were knifed and fell, that would be the end to it; no one would be able to get down into the Canyon at this point to find out what had killed him or caused him to fall.

The morning was hot, yet seemed cold.

The first speaker said, "Look to your right, Dawlish, where the catsclaw makes a horseshoe."

Dawlish looked downwards and to the right, as if the Canyon compelled him to obey. He saw tiny bushes, looking no larger than tufts of grass but actually as high as his waist, hundreds of feet below; it was roughly in the shape of a horseshoe. He waited for more instructions while his mind began to work, to twist this way and that for a way out of the trap. Then he stopped thinking, for he saw the shape; the skull and bones and clothes.

The man behind him was much closer.

"See what I mean, Dawlish?"

There was little doubt that the skeleton was Bill Newton's. There it lay, amid the silence; and there was none other with it.

"A thing like that can happen again," the man said. He sounded as if he were in the open, but Dawlish did not look round. The still shape held his gaze—and in his mind's eye he saw a second. "It can happen quick and easy. You can't get away. You're covered from every side except the big hole and you won't get any help from there. Why did you come, Dawlish?"

Dawlish said slowly, "As if you didn't know."

He turned round.

The man was in sight, ten feet away from him, with a gun in his right hand pointing towards the ground; but he had plenty of time to level it and shoot before Dawlish could reach him. It was a small man whom Dawlish did not think he had seen before, and whom he probably wouldn't recognize again. A Stetson pulled low over his eyes put the top half of his face into deep shadow; a scarf, tied round his face from the bridge of his nose downwards, hid the rest. He wore grey slacks, a brown shirt and brown shoes with thick crêpe soles. There was a slit in the scarf, which enabled him to breathe more freely and to talk without difficulty.

"Don't talk back. Why did you come?"

"I came to find my wife."

The man said: "Why did *she* come? Who sent you?"

There was no answer but a new element had come, almost as unreal as everything that had gone before. Felicity had seized a chance to drive across the States, stopping wherever her fancy pleased; no one had sent her anywhere. Dawlish could say so but wouldn't be believed. He stood silent, staring at the hidden face, seeing the gun so loosely held but knowing that he hadn't a chance to get at his own. And if he had, there were the other men, one with a knife-throwing act that hadn't yet been properly demonstrated.

"Just answer a simple question," the man said. "Who sent you?"

Dawlish drew a deep breath.

"Just answer a simple question. Where's my wife?"

The first effect was like a blast of cold air on a man who has a chance to give it; Felicity was dead. Once he had thought, 'if she were dead' and now, for a swift and hateful second, he believed that she was. And he hated. He hated the man in front of him and the invisible men behind, and if he could have reached the one, he would have killed and not cared what happened to him afterwards.

Then the man said, "You won't see her again until you've talked."

The first effect was like a blast of cold air on a man who has been standing in steam heat for hours. Dawlish actually moved back a pace, as if driven by the blast. Then the hot air of fear and despair blew fiercely again. Of course the man would say that, would make him think that Felicity was alive; what other chance was there of making Dawlish talk?

"Why are we wasting time?" Dawlish asked heavily. "When I've got her back, even when I've seen her alive, I'll talk."

"You'll talk before that," the man said. "Or else you'll fall into the big hole, and then *she'll* talk. She's being softened up now."

Was this a lie? Hope that Felicity was alive came in a blinding flash, lifting up his spirits, filling him with new, fierce purpose—to make this man talk. "Just let me see her," Dawlish said.

"Take it easy." Perhaps his eyes burned into the man and worried him; his voice sharpened. "Who sent you, Dawlish?"

Dawlish didn't answer. The man slowly raised his gun. Done that way, it didn't really seem like a threat, but none could have been more menacing. The gun stopped when the muzzle covered Dawlish's stomach; not his chest—and as it stopped another flash of dazzling light passed in front of Dawlish's eyes.

This time the knife did not clatter against a rock, just vanished into silence. Dawlish stopped, as if turned into stone itself. The small man in front of him bent down, picked up a rock about the size of a tennis ball, and tossed it towards Dawlish. Dawlish ducked, but there was no need, it went over his head as the man had intended.

There followed an agony of silence as it went down and down.

"It's a long way to the bottom," the man said. "Make it easy for yourself, Dawlish. Who sent you? If you make it the hard way, you'll come with us and we won't let you go."

He wanted an answer; and if he wanted it so badly, would he kill?

Dawlish turned his back on him, slowly. He was less than five feet from the Canyon's rim. There was no protection. Hundreds of feet below was the first formation of rock, hardened by millions of years, covered with the cruel catsclaw which would rip the flesh off a man's bones. He went a step nearer, and the man called:

"Listen to reason, Dawlish. You can't get away from us. Talk now and we'll fade. If you don't, we'll take you with us and you won't get away. You've a chance and your wife's got a chance. Who sent you?"

There was the urgency of alarm in the man, at some element which he didn't understand. Dawlish, ignoring him, went right to the edge and peered over. The rock below seemed to draw him; he set his teeth. He scanned it, right and left. Twenty yards away from him an outcrop jutted out of the side of the Canyon, with a ledge which looked small but was probably three or four feet wide; the rest of the Canyon wall was sheer. He looked the other way again as the man said harshly:

"Dawlish!"

Dawlish looked back to the outcrop. If he started above it, he might be able to get down to the ledge. He could turn his back on the Canyon, lower himself, hang at full length—some eight feet or a little more. The ledge couldn't be more than twenty feet below the rim, and the rock looked solid. He might be able to climb down. They thought he could give them information that mattered, and wouldn't kill; if he were wrong about that, this was his big, his last mistake. He moved slowly towards the rim above the ledge, and the man called again:

"You haven't a chance. Tell me——"

Dawlish turned sharply, his face hard as the rock itself, his eyes glittering as brightly as the steel blades which had flashed across them.

"So you want to know who sent me. I'll tell you. When my wife is back at the hotel."

"You'll play it our way!" That new element, born of Dawlish's manner, made the voice hoarse. The gun levelled at Dawlish's chest was held more tightly, all nonchalance was gone. "If you go over there you'll end up the way Newton ended up."

His urgency proved that he didn't want that yet.

"And you'll hang," Dawlish said. "Or do they electrocute you in Arizona?" He moved as he spoke, edging towards the rim above the ledge. The sun burned more fiercely than ever; it was viciously hot. Another car hummed along the road, not far away, and faded again; the silence took possession. Dawlish could not be sure of his exact position, so he turned and looked; two more yards and he would be directly above the ledge.

He expected another frightening knife, waited for it, and saw it come. He swerved to one side and it went past him and over and dropped into the silence.

"If you want to know who sent me," Dawlish said clearly, "I shouldn't do that again."

They wanted to know; and they wanted to stop whatever he was planning to do. Perhaps they didn't understand it; perhaps they were sure that there wasn't a chance, that the ledge wouldn't hold him. He went down on his knees.

"You stay where you are," the small man said; he spoke oddly, breathlessly. "Just stay where you are. You won't get hurt if you tell us who sent you. Just name them. You'll get your wife back——"

Dawlish put a knee over the Canyon's rim. Below, the skeleton of Bill Newton lay spread-eagled; below, the silence was like the stillness of death. The man up here didn't know what to do—and did not want to kill him. Later, Dawlish could exult about that. A single shot would kill; or a knife, well aimed. They might decide to kill, after all.

Dawlish could not, dared not hurry. He felt a jutting rock beneath his right foot, went over, found another lower down; he stood one-footed on that, head on a level with the ground, staring into the covered face of the man with the gun. Two other men appeared, farther away, coming forward slowly as if hypnotized. Neither was masked, but their faces were vague in the shade of their Stetsons.

"Dawlish, you'll kill yourself."

"Just send my wife back to the hotel," said Dawlish.

He dropped to his full length, large hands gripping the rocky rim. He hung for a moment and looked down. He could just see the ledge, but it seemed tiny against the vastness of the yawning valley. There were rocks for his feet to rest on, others for his hands. He began to climb down. He found some support but no firm grasp. If he slipped, it would be his last slip. He stared upwards. No one appeared. They would be watching, from the right or the left. He stretched his right foot downwards, groping for the ledge. He seemed to have been clinging to the side of the Canyon for an eternity, and his foot touched nothing. He moved his head again and looked downwards; the ledge was there, it couldn't be more than three feet beneath his foot. He lowered himself so slowly that he hardly seemed to move, and the sun burned the back of his head.

He touched the ledge.

He looked up; to the right, he saw a hat, perhaps a pair of eyes; that was all. He looked down. The ledge was wider than he had thought, he could take a walk on it! Exhilaration, with its unsuspected dangers, replaced terror. He turned round quickly. He was in the middle of the ledge, with two or three feet on either side of him, at least four in front of him, and it seemed solid enough to hold a tank. He leaned back, filled with a relief too great to allow thought or any other feeling; but it ebbed, slowly, and thought came back.

Rather than kill him, they had let him climb down here; that was how badly they wanted to know who had sent him. Now they would be sure that someone had. If Felicity were alive, they would keep her alive.

If Felicity . . .

Then, only then, he began to wonder what chance there was of being found and rescued.

CHAPTER VIII

THE ROPE

SOMEONE would come. There were tourists, hundreds of them, one party or another would come to this point, the Big Rock would surely invite them. When he heard voices he would shout, and if shouting failed he would shoot. Someone would *have* to come. He took the gun out of his hip pocket and placed it in his coat pocket. The cloth of his coat was hot to touch. The sun on his head and face seemed fiercer than he had ever known the sun to be. The few square feet of the ledge seemed to creep in on him, growing smaller. How long would he be able to last out here, with that sun pouring down, drawing the blood to his head?

If Felicity were alive, and this meant a chance to find her, he could stay here for ever.

Why hadn't Morgan taken some precaution; one man, even two, could have been trusted?

His mouth was clammy yet dry. He wanted to smoke a cigarette but knew that it would make him drier. He took out a pack of Pall Mall, nearly full, and looked at the red paper, then put it back. He told himself that he was relaxing, yet actually in constant tension. He heard fancied sounds, the true song of the birds, a rustling which might be from the wind or from some creeping animal. At first he took no notice of time; when at last he looked at his watch, it was nearly eleven o'clock.

He started up, and banged his head against the wall; was that a shout? Everything else faded from his mind as he strained his ears.

Was it?

He raised his hands slightly, and opened his mouth—and then heard it again. Someone was shouting, not far away; it couldn't be far away, could it? He stood up slowly; and there was a risk of falling if he took a single false step. Upright, he listened, almost praying—and the next shout was nearer.

He took out his gun and fired down into the Canyon. The shot roared, echoed, roared again. There was no answering shot, nothing to suggest that he had been heard, but after a few seconds a voice called:

"*Daw-lish!*"

"I'm here!" he roared.

Silence followed, but it was hopeful and soon broken by voices which were much nearer.

Dawlish drew in his breath.

"I'm—here! Beneath—the—Big—Rock."

He paused between the words, to make each clearer; and then a shout came so quickly that he thought it was an answer. He waited. Soon he heard voices of men who were talking among themselves. He stared upwards, and saw a bare head appear over the rim of the Canyon, turned towards him; then an arm waved. He waved back, and leaned against the wall of the Canyon, grinning with the dizzy marvel of relief.

Next time he looked up, a rope was being lowered over the rim.

• • • • •

The only familiar face was Elliott's. Half a dozen men, presumably Park rangers, were with him.

Dawlish emptied a water-bottle, gasped as he finished, and took out his cigarettes. No one had asked him a single question that mattered, and Elliott obviously didn't intend to. The Deputy Warden, like his men, looked almost part of the rugged land, daylight turned his face into one carved out of rock, and gave his eyes a brightness and a calmness which came from looking into long distances.

"We'll go back in my car," he said, told his men to follow, and walked with Dawlish towards the road thirty yards from the Big Rock. He had a green Ford sedan, parked in the shade of a taller tree than most. He opened the door for Dawlish, then took the wheel, but didn't switch on the engine.

"I had a man following you," he said simply. "He was attacked, and tied up. Others were watching through glasses from several view-points. We came as soon as we could."

"Sooner than I expected," Dawlish said. "Where's Morgan?"

"In Williams. He has other work to do," Elliott added, and it was obvious that the tension of the search had dried up his humour. "When you're ready to talk, tell me what happened." He turned on the ignition and started the engine.

"There were three men," Dawlish said heavily. "They've a queer idea. And they told me that my wife was alive."

• • • • •

Daylight made little difference to Hal Morgan. He was just about the thinnest man Dawlish had ever seen, and his face was a mass of wrinkles, like cracked leather. Was he as old as he looked? That would make him venerable; but there was youth and vitality in his eyes, he gave an impression of restrained vigour as he moved, even as he sat listening. By then drinks had been sent up.

Dawlish finished the second telling and knew what questions to expect. Morgan didn't let it wait for long.

"And they kept asking who sent you, Dawlish?"

"Yes."

Morgan asked mildly. "Who did?"

"No one sent me. No one sent my wife."

"Well, there's one good thing, they've come into the open," Morgan mused. "Last night we were guessing at something like this and this morning we know. You've helped that much, Dawlish. If you could describe these guys you'd help more."

"I can't—not enough to matter. One was very small, the two others Morkel-size. They were careful not to show their faces enough for me to see. They'll try again," Dawlish added softly, "they're sure to try again. And they'll know that I've had this session with you, Sheriff."

"The real puzzle comes in right there," Morgan said. "They think someone sent you and want to know who it was so bad that they've taken this risk—attacked one of Wilf's men and made an open attack on you. What would you do next, if you had your way, Dawlish?"

"I'd find a way of letting them know I haven't told you a thing," Dawlish said. "The best way would be to go and see Trig Clay." His gaze was level on Morgan's eyes.

"Now I wonder why you would do a thing like that." Morgan was wide-eyed for once.

"To make them think I don't give a damn what happens about Newton's death; all I want is my wife."

"I can understand it," Morgan conceded, "but there are things about you I can't understand, Dawlish."

"If I tell you that I was with M.I.5 during the war and for a while afterwards, it might help you to see what makes me tick."

After a long pause, Morgan said slowly: "I guess I'm beginning to see what makes you tick."

"So you've been an agent, Dawlish, and you've been accustomed to working on your own, I guess. "Is that what you're doing now, Dawlish? A lone-wolf act for M.I.5?"

Dawlish said gently, "It is not."

"You'd deny it, even if it were."

"I can't make you believe it, but you know everything I can tell you."

"I hope that's right," said Morgan, and smiled as if he were beginning to believe that it was. "How do you like it, Wilf, we've a one-time Secret Service ace with us. No wonder he's so strong-willed! It could explain the big mystery, Dawlish, if you look at it the right way. Don't tell me you haven't thought of how."

"I've thought of how," Dawlish agreed. "You hear that I was with M.I.5 and jump to the conclusion that I'm working for the Branch now. If the other folk connected me with M.I.5 they might jump to the same conclusion. It's going to be a long time before I'm convinced of it."

"Maybe. It's going to be a long time before I like the implications behind it," Morgan said. "Why should these folk worry about a man from England even if he has a Secret Service record? If we could answer that, maybe we could answer a lot of other things—including why Bill Newton was killed and why your wife was kidnapped, friend. Do you really believe she's alive now?"

"There's a chance. They could have a reason for keeping her alive. They could have a stronger reason for wanting to make me believe that she is," Dawlish added abruptly. "I'm going to let them think I do, for the time being."

Elliott said quietly, "Through Trig Clay?"

"Who else?"

There was a long pause. Morgan looked as if he were trying to see into Dawlish's mind for the truth. Then he said abruptly:

"How do you want to play it, Dawlish?"

"As we've started. I'll go and see Trig Clay. I'll tell him you've been questioning me since I came out of the Canyon but I haven't told you a thing that matters. I'll make him believe I'm playing this my own way but I can't help it if you watch me. You think that my wife's disappearance is connected with Bill Newton's death and you're very anxious to find her. I can't be sure that Clay will believe me, but it's worth trying."

After another long pause, Morgan said: "Let me tell you one little thing. If a man is called Trig it could have something to do with his trigger-finger. Do you carry a gun?"

"What I need," said Dawlish, "is a shoulder holster."

CHAPTER IX

TRIG CLAY

IT WAS half past one.

Dawlish drove slowly. Soon he reached the first of the shacks. There were hundreds of them, built beneath fir trees, getting some shade. Families sat outside them eating in the open.

Trig Clay's shack was Number 204. It stood some distance from the road; most of the nearby shacks were closed, and Clay's door was shut but a bright blue Packard stood outside it, nose pointing towards the log walls. No sound came from the shack. Dawlish knocked and stood back, expecting Clay to open the door, his expression almost amiable; the shocks could come to Clay later.

The shock came to Dawlish.

A woman opened the door.

If she had been fashioned and moulded, polished and finished off for the single purpose of attracting the male, it couldn't have been a better job. She wasn't so much beautiful as luscious. Even the shade inside the shack couldn't dull all the lights in her flaming red hair. She had a smooth, creamy complexion, huge green eyes, and her lips glistened with lipstick which kept to the natural shape because that couldn't be improved on.

She wore a two-piece swim-suit of emerald green with a filmy wrap over her shoulders, hiding little; nothing was meant to be hidden. The skin at arms and shoulders, legs and waist, had a golden hue; she looked flawless; and because she was surprised, perhaps disappointed, her lips parted and she showed teeth that were fine and shining bright.

"Why, hallo," she greeted. That was all the time it took for her disappointment to fade. She looked Dawlish up and down and obviously she liked what she saw. Her teeth showed now in a smile as if she meant to make sure that Dawlish also liked what he saw.

"Good afternoon," said Dawlish. "Is Mr. Clay in?"

"He's not, right now. I thought you were the man himself," she said brightly. "Why don't you wait a while, he won't be that long."

"I'd like to."

"It's cooler inside," she said.

It wasn't very much cooler. The room was small, with a table, three upright chairs, two wooden rocking-chairs, a skin rug. The walls were of rough pine, the floor of polished pine. Several photographs were pinned to the wall, all of this woman; she seemed to be wearing more now than in any of the pictures.

"Why don't you sit down?" she asked, and touched a chair. "You're English, aren't you?"

Dawlish grinned. "I guess so!"

"Oh, don't try to talk our way," she pleaded, and sat on the corner of the table, very close to him. "I just love to hear an Englishman talk the way he does at home. Say, wait a minute, can I get you some coffee? Or a drink, maybe?"

"Coffee would be just right."

"I'll get it right now." She slid off the table and disappeared into another room—the only other room. He saw the foot of a bed, and a dressing-table. He leaned back in the rocker and closed his eyes, although the room was shady; perhaps she had been right, and it was cooler. He heard cups clinking. She wouldn't be long, and in the little time he had to work in, he had to decide what line to take. A woman was a woman, all the world over, and he didn't think he was misjudging her in thinking that she wasn't exactly a one-man woman—but just now, she was Trig Clay's.

She was moving about the other room. Dawlish stood up and looked at one of the photographs. It was a professional job, and the name on it was stamped, not signed: Eloise. He moved to another photograph, signed in ink, and was there when she came in.

"Don't look at those, they're terrible."

Dawlish turned round, smiling. "It's a waste of time with the original here with me."

She laughed and put down two cups of coffee on the table. Two wrapped lumps of sugar were in each saucer.

"Trig didn't tell me he had an English friend," she said, "I think that was mean of him." She leaned forward, with a cup of coffee held out to him. She was a Juno, with a tiny waist and full, provocative breasts, and she looked as if she had a naive joy of living. "Have you come to look at the Canyon?"

"I was told I mustn't miss it."

"It sure has something," agreed Eloise, "but I'm not like Trig, he likes to come and see it three or four times each year. It's too quiet around here for that—don't you agree?"

"It's certainly quiet."

"Give me the big city," Eloise said. She sat on the table, twisting her legs round one of the legs, the wrap tossed back from her body so that it covered only her shoulders. She had a quality which was more typically American in Dawlish's eyes than anything else he had found, it was true of nearly everyone he met. This woman was herself; she said what she thought; she could talk to him as if they were old friends, there were no apparent reticences, no false diffidence. She enjoyed life if she could get it the way she liked it. She enjoyed sitting opposite a man who was massive as well as striking, and she wanted him to like her; and she showed that. It seemed to Dawlish that it was as simple as that.

"I hope you like your coffee that way, I don't think I've ever served coffee to an Englishman before."

Dawlish sipped.

"Just right," he said. "Now I know that my friends are right."

"Say that again."

He laughed. "They call me lucky."

"You can't get any place without some luck," she said, with a kind of gay seriousness. "You just have to have it. It runs swell for a while, and then it dries up on you. What I say is, take it with both hands when you've got it, and when it dries up, go out and look for some more."

"Try to tell me a better way," Dawlish said lightly.

"There just isn't one."

"I think I agree with you. Does Trig Clay bring you luck?"

She shrugged. "Trig's okay," she said, and the lack of enthusiasm might be genuine but was as likely to be calculated to fool Dawlish. "You known Trig long?"

"We haven't met yet."

"He's got a habit of saying you never know what's coming next," said Eloise lightly. "You see how right he is."

"It's good to be right sometimes."

"Oh, sure. We're old buddies, Trig and me. Once we did an act together, but Trig had everything except what it takes." The merriment glowed from her eyes. "I guess he just didn't like the stage, and looked around for something that would pay off better."

"I hope he found it."

"I guess he must have," she said. She wasn't likely to tell him more than that, even if she knew any more. "Why do we have to sit here and talk about Trig? You want to tell me about yourself. Maybe you've got a name?"

He grinned. "Dawlish."

"Dawlish what?"

"Pat Dawlish."

"I thought all Pats were Irish."

"You must blame my grandmother."

"You see, I'm learning about you, you've an Irish grandmother," Eloise said, and seemed to gurgle. She gripped the table with both hands and leaned towards him. "How long have you been in the States and how do you like it? I guess everyone asks you that and you know just how to fool them!"

"A week, and I like it. New York——"

"Gee, New York isn't *America*."

"I can't imagine finding it in any other country," Dawlish said dryly.

"Well, maybe not. Did you fly here?" The questions might be as lightly personal as they seemed; or she might be probing, ready to tell Clay all she had learned.

"No, I drove from New York."

"You couldn't have spent long in New York," said Eloise, "but how right you were to come out West. The East hasn't got a thing we haven't got better on the West Coast. How long will you be staying?"

"I don't know yet." Dawlish shrugged.

He heard a sound outside but didn't glance towards the door; he expected it to open or someone to knock. Neither happened. He was wary from then on. Questions tumbled out of the girl, he answered them easily but was conscious all the time that someone else might be listening, and the someone would be Clay. He judged that five minutes passed, and then the sound was repeated and this time Eloise heard it. She glanced round at the door. It opened slowly, so slowly that

Dawlish found himself stiffening, raised his hand so that it could slide towards the gun in the shoulder holster quickly.

Trig Clay came in.

He had both hands in sight; Dawlish let his fall to the arms of his chair. Clay wasn't so much big as thickset and powerful. He wore the wide-brimmed hat, a cream-coloured shirt with the sleeves ending just above the elbow, and pale blue pants. His face was as dark as seasoned oak, and his eyes, a dull grey, seemed to take the life out of him, made him like a robot. His mouth was flat and seemed to have no shape; the long jaw and the small nose made him almost ugly, full-face.

Dawlish sensed the change which came over the girl. She slid off the table, and shot a startled, almost frightened glance at Dawlish; she knew Clay wasn't pleased to see him.

"Why, Trig, we've been waiting——"

"I can see you've been waiting." The clipped voice brought back the scene on the rim path the night before. "You can find some other place to wait, beautiful, not right here."

"Why, sure, Trig." He could easily frighten her. She moved swiftly towards the bedroom.

"And not right there."

"I'm just getting myself a wrap," Eloise said defensively. Her startled, almost frightened glance swept over Dawlish again. He wasn't sure that she was as scared as she wanted him to believe.

So far, Clay had taken no notice of Dawlish, behaved as if he weren't in the small room. He watched the girl, the door when she disappeared, and his eyes remained dull when she came out, wearing a cotton wrap and carrying a linen bag. "See you," she said, as she passed; and she didn't say anything to Dawlish.

The door closed behind her.

Dawlish hadn't moved from his chair. He still smiled, amiably, almost inanely. With the door closed, Clay turned to look at him. Clay believed in creating effect without words. He didn't speak, just stared. The silence became almost the silence of the Canyon, each man determined that the other should speak first. Clay stood with his arms hanging straight by his side; he didn't seem to carry a gun, but the cream shirt was of heavy linen and bulky beneath the shoulders; there was probably one there. He looked powerful enough to be a professional strong man; and his eyes were the eyes of a man from whom all life had been drained.

Dawlish put his arms on the arms of his chair, and began to get up. Clay, three feet away from him, pushed out a hand, flattened it against Dawlish's chest and pushed him back. The chair rocked. Dawlish let it steady and began again; Clay kept his arms by his side, as if waiting for the moment when Dawlish was almost upright to push him down. He waited too long. Dawlish leapt at him.

CHAPTER X

STRUGGLE

ALARM came too late to save Clay from the first leap. Dawlish smashed a clenched left fist into the long jaw, knocked the man sideways, then rammed his right fist into Clay's stomach; the blow didn't land as he meant it to, Clay was quick. He took part of the blow on his arm, and kicked. If they had been face to face, he would have caught Dawlish between the legs. Instead he kicked against Dawlish's thigh.

Two could fight rough. Dawlish bent his knee and brought it up into Clay's stomach; Clay didn't do anything to save himself from that, but it didn't flatten him.

He thrust his arms forward, linked his hands behind Dawlish's neck and jerked Dawlish's head forward, then his fingers clawed into the flesh as he struggled for a grip. He had long arms and long fingers; those fingers might have been wire rope, and could be deadly. Dawlish brought his forehead down with all his weight on to Clay's nose, and it did more damage than the knee. Clay relaxed, backed, tried to get clear.

Dawlish followed up, bent down, grabbed Clay's right wrist, twisted and heaved. The man went over his back, crashed against the wall and thudded down. The shack sounded as if it were falling to pieces.

Clay was trying to pick himself up. There was blood at his mouth. His right arm lay limp, he was levering himself from the floor with his left. Dawlish bent double, took a grip round his knees, lifted him so that his head hung downwards, held him upside down, then sent him toppling. Any ordinary man —most men—would have been finished. Clay wasn't.

He leapt at Dawlish, trying to clutch Dawlish round the knees, but one arm wasn't enough. He missed and fell. Dawlish picked him up by the waist and hurled him against the wall. The shack seemed to shake and break up. Clay hit the wall and slithered down, knocking a chair over as he fell. His eyes were still open but the will to fight had gone.

Dawlish took a step towards him.

The door burst open. Dawlish didn't know and didn't care who was behind him. He took another step.

He felt something brush against his side, heard gasping breath. Then Eloise thrust herself in front of Clay, hands stretched out to fend Dawlish off. In her eyes was a fine simulation of terror; it certainly wasn't real, but an act. She backed so that her feet touched the fallen man.

"Get to hell out of here!" she screeched at Dawlish.

Dawlish stopped, and backed a pace. He could still see Clay's eyes and the fire of hate in them. He took a small automatic out of his pocket. Eloise seemed not to notice.

"Take his gun out of his shoulder holster," Dawlish ordered.

"Get your big hulk out of here!"

Dawlish moved forward, his speed bewildering her. He thrust her aside, and as she moved, he bent down swiftly, ripped Clay's shirt open and made buttons fly off. The gun was there in the shoulder holster. Dawlish took it out and backed away. Eloise turned her back on him, dropped on her knees beside Clay, took his left hand between hers.

"God! What has he done? Trig, what——"

"Eloise," said Dawlish quietly, "this isn't the right place for you. The fighting's over, Clay and I are going to have a little talk. Come back in half an hour, and if you haven't had training in first-aid, find someone who has. Hurry."

She stared down at Clay as if for orders. He didn't speak but nodded at the door. She got up and went slowly towards it.

Clay made an effort. "Stay out," he rasped, "and keep your mouth shut."

She closed the door.

Dawlish went to it, opened it and looked outside; no one else appeared to have heard the struggle. Eloise stood against a tree a few yards off, looking at him; another time he could worry about the way she looked, try to guess what was going on in her mind. She had stopped being naive, she was all the cunning of women in one seductive body.

Dawlish closed the door again. It had a wooden bar to fasten it, as well as a lock. He dropped the bar into position. No one could see in from the windows because the venetian blinds were down. He turned towards Clay, who was dragging himself to his feet. Dawlish sat where Eloise had, on the table, his back against the wall. Clay reached his feet, but was unsteady. Dawlish didn't speak. Clay moved slowly, one step at a time, until he reached an upright chair. He lowered himself into it, and his right arm still hung limp by his side.

"Where is she?" asked Dawlish.

Clay spoke as if the words hurt him.

"Who told you she was alive?"

It wasn't a sneer. It seemed to Dawlish a simple question with nothing tied to it. He could answer, once the pain of the tear in his mind had subsided, but he didn't.

"She's alive," he said. "You needed to keep her alive."

"So that's your guess. Okay, keep guessing. I saw her ten days ago. They were getting tired of holding her. I don't think they would hold her ten more days."

Dawlish's eyes were as dull as Clay's.

"Where was she?"

"I can't tell you that much. It was a shack among the redwoods, not so far from Highway 101. An old lumber mill. It isn't used for that now. I was taken there by car and brought away by car, both times at night. You can believe it or you can do the other thing."

It looked as if Clay had decided that the wise thing was to talk; but his spirit wasn't crushed, it was just that he knew he hadn't a chance and didn't intend to suffer for stubbornness which wouldn't get him anywhere. He might be lying; he probably was.

"Who took you?" Dawlish asked.

"Some guy."

Dawlish said, "Don't make the mistake of thinking that is funny, Clay."

"I know when a thing's funny and I know when a man's in killing mood," Clay said. "One day I'll kill you." That came out flatly, as if Clay didn't give a thought to the possibility that the day might never come. "Some guy took me. I haven't seen him since."

"I'll let it pass. Who did you talk to last night after you'd followed me to Newton's house and back?"

Clay wasn't surprised; probably he had already guessed how he had been identified. He dragged the back of his left hand across his lips, and smeared it with blood. He looked as if he would never be whole again.

"That is the guy who paid me for watching you, paid me for watching your wife and Newton. He's the guy who will have to hire someone else to work for him. I'm through. I don't know anyone else in the racket. He's at the hotel and maybe he has others with him—I wouldn't know but I can guess. He's a guy who doesn't let his right hand know what his left hand is doing."

"Doesn't he have a name?"

"He has a name," Clay said.

"What does he look like?"

"He's just a little guy with a face like a thousand other little guys. Dark hair, dark skin. I don't know any more."

He meant, "I won't talk any more."

"Is he registered at the hotel?"

"I didn't ask him."

"When do you expect to see him again?"

"Maybe today, maybe next year, maybe never. When he knows what has happened to me, he won't want to stall around. Why don't you take a powder?"

There were men who could be broken and made to talk. Clay wasn't one of them. He had one purpose in what he had said: to make Dawlish think that he had worked for someone else. He was hurt but he wasn't frightened, wasn't just trying to get out of trouble, simply trying to put Dawlish on the wrong track; it might be a good move to let him think he had succeeded. Smashing him up even more wouldn't get Dawlish anywhere. Yet.

"I didn't bring any powder with me," Dawlish said, and he wasn't trying to be funny. "This man will see you again. You can give him a message from me. Tell him that if my wife isn't returned to the hotel, I'll go to Sheriff Morgan and tell him all I know. That includes the real reason why I jumped into the Canyon this morning."

Clay exclaimed, "You did *what*?"

If he hadn't heard about what had happened during the morning, it suggested that he might have been telling the truth about the rest. He had pointed a finger at a man he wouldn't name, and that might be all he would do. Dawlish watched him, sensing the pain at his mouth, in his arm, in the rest of his body.

"I didn't jump far," Dawlish said. "The rangers found me and Morgan wanted to know how I got down there. I stalled. I stalled for one reason—because I've come here to get my wife back, and I don't think much of the police. But if I change my mind, if I come round to thinking that she's dead, I'll tell Morgan everything. I'll name you and everyone else I can. Tell your friend not to make any mistake."

He stood up, Clay watching with those lack-lustre eyes. He went into the bedroom, collected three suites, two suit-cases and a small folio case. He brought them into the small room, went through the pockets of the suits, found nothing he thought would help, went through the suit-cases and the folio case; there was nothing in any of them that he was likely to be able to use. Clay didn't look interested, just in pain. Dawlish went back into the other room; there were few places to hide anything, and he doubted whether anything that mattered was hidden.

Then he saw a slip of paper with a scrawl on it, tucked beneath an ash-tray on the dressing-table. It said:

K–98, and beneath this a list: *Toothpaste—grapes—cigs—service auto—D*–119—*E can get gas.*

D–119; or Dawlish in Room 119. Then K was probably a man in Room 98. This could really be something.

Dawlish didn't move the slip but rejoined Clay, who hadn't shifted his position.

"I won't use gloves next time," he said. "I'm coming back."

Clay didn't answer.

CHAPTER XI

ADVICE

DAWLISH did not drive straight back to the hotel, but drove to Angel Lodge and telephoned Morkel, who was eager, anxious to be helpful.

"Who's in Room 98, Mr. Dawlish? I'll find out right now; just wait, please." He wasn't gone long. "It's a Mr. Elias Kramer, Mr. Dawlish. Does he come into this?"

"He could," Dawlish said. "Will you tell Morgan he might be worth watching?"

"Surely."

"Thanks."

There were other things Dawlish wanted to do, but the first was to find out whether he had been followed. He drove out along the rim in the opposite direction from the one he had taken during the morning. The road seldom gave a clear view of the Canyon, but there were several view-points, each with its group of cars, and people wandering off the road towards the Canyon's edge. Dawlish joined none of them until he had reached the end of the rim-drive. There were more cars and two buses.

He got out.

No car had followed him, and no one here appeared to be interested in him. He saw two of Elliott's men, one of whom had been among the rescue party that morning. The man grinned as he caught sight of Dawlish and made a thumbs-up sign. Dawlish waved. A guide turned away, at the head of a group of tourists, and began to talk about the Canyon; there was enthusiasm in his slow, almost singsong Texan voice.

Dawlish drove quickly back to the hotel, left the car outside and asked if Mr. Kramer had been seen to leave the hotel. The room clerk said in surprise:

"Why, sure, he's just checked out."

"You sure?"

"He drove off not five minutes ago," the clerk said.

So Dawlish knew that he had put the wrong thing first. K for Kramer was on his way out. It was doubtful whether Morgan had had time to get on his trail, but Morgan wouldn't lose much time, could trace the man—but then what? Kramer must have been told what had happened to Clay and been in a hurry to disappear in case his turn came next. That was logical but it didn't give the police any reason to hold him.

If he, Dawlish, had come straight here from Clay's shack . . .

Well, he hadn't. A mistake was a mistake. He had lost twenty minutes, perhaps half an hour; and might have lost a lead to Felicity. But he had a name to work on.

He asked what Kramer looked like.

"Just another guy, Mr. Dawlish. A little guy, with dark hair and kind of sallow."

That fitted Clay's description.

"Thanks," Dawlish said.

"You're welcome. Say, there's a message for you. A lady called."

Dawlish caught his breath. But no, it wouldn't happen this way, Clay or Kramer or whoever held Felicity wouldn't do exactly what he was told; not yet.

"Who?"

"Mrs. Newton," the clerk said. "She left this message."

"Oh, thanks." Dawlish went to the door, opening a sealed envelope. He could imagine that Marion Newton would want to see him again; he was quite sure that he didn't want to see her yet.

The note was a brief scrawl:

Just to say how much your visit helped me. I'm going into my sister-in-law's with Judy to stay for a few days, and called in hoping I could say good-bye. Thanks ever so.

Dawlish slipped the note into his pocket and went upstairs, but not to his own room. Number 98 was off another passage. A Hopi walked softly, impassively past him. He reached Kramer's room when the passage was empty; and used a skeleton key. He opened the door and stepped inside swiftly.

The room hadn't been cleaned yet. The bed was made but the clothes were rumpled, as if the man had lain on top of them, resting. There was an empty bottle of bourbon, a bowl of ice which had nearly all melted, and several screwed-up cigarette packets—*Camels*—in or on the floor by the waste-paper basket. There were other screws of paper. He smoothed these out, and found them to be all the same; the opening sentences of a letter.

I can't get anything, one began, without any courtesy 'Dear anyone'. The next said, *I guess it's time we . . .* and stopped there. The last read, *You'll find me back home . . .* and that was all.

So Kramer, who had a big, gaudy handwriting, had hardly known what to say, how to start; he had been writing to tell someone he was on his way.

There was nothing else of interest. Dawlish put the smoothed-out papers in his pocket, and slipped out of the room, going straight to his own.

As he reached it, Clay's threat to kill came to his mind; if

Clay had meant anything, he had meant that. From this moment on, Dawlish had to be on watch minute by minute—as careful as if Felicity were waiting for him at home, praying that he wouldn't take wild chances. He turned the key in the lock softly, but it made a little noise. He took the key out and didn't open the door immediately; waited several seconds, then turned the handle and thrust the door wide open.

The room was empty; and chaotic.

• • • • •

Dawlish did not look about the room, just took the state of chaos in at a single glance, then watched the open door of the bathroom. Nothing seemed to move. He approached the door stealthily, from one side, and peered through the crack between the door and the wall. He satisfied himself that the bathroom was empty.

He turned back to the bedroom.

His two cases had been forced open, the contents flung out, the lining ripped open. The bed had been stripped and the mattress was pushed to one side. Everything had been moved and left in the wrong place, or upside down; it was so thoroughly done that it was almost too thorough; no one searching need have made such a mess unless they had wanted to.

There had been nothing to find; so they could have found nothing.

The telephone-bell rang.

He had only to stretch out an arm to reach it. He took off the receiver, speculating. Elliott? Morgan? He said:

"Hallo?"

"Mr. Dawlish?" It was a man with a voice he didn't recognize except now he knew that it was the voice of a man from the East, like Clay, not from the West, like Morgan or Elliott.

"Yes."

"I'm told you're looking for something," the man said. He didn't hurry, didn't put any emphasis into his voice. "Look harder. Look under the bed, pal. You asked for it back, didn't you?"

The man rang off.

Dawlish stood with the receiver in his hand, staring at the bed. The mattress was still awry, but he couldn't see under it. There was hardly room for anyone to be beneath it; was there?

The casual words had torn at his nerves, started the dynamo pulsing. He'd told the trio, and told Clay, to send Felicity to the hotel. "You asked for it back, didn't you?" "Look under the bed, pal." He put the receiver down slowly. Reason didn't come into it, he was beyond reason. He moved, put a hand beneath the edge of the bed and heaved.

The bed stood on its side.

The wood floor was beneath—nothing else. Well, nothing much; there was a folded newspaper. He bent down slowly and picked it up. It wasn't only a newspaper, something else was between the folds. He took it to the writing-table, unfolding it slowly, his teeth clamped together. Then he saw what was inside, and he almost choked.

Drawn through a platinum wedding-ring, and tied to it, was a long lock of hair.

It was between-coloured hair; like Felicity's. There were a few strands of grey; like Felicity's. He held his breath as he looked more closely at the wedding-ring, chased on the outer edge; like Felicity's. It was hers; there wasn't any doubt, the ring clinched it. Her hair and her wedding-ring, their bond. He held it tightly between his fingers, and then his gaze fell on the page in which it had been folded—the picture page of a Los Angeles newspaper. He stood so still that he might have been frozen into stiffness. One of the pictures was of a woman, hanging behind a door; dead.

The woman's name didn't matter, nor did the circumstances; there was just the implication and the threat.

The telephone-bell rang.

Dawlish looked across the room and moved slowly towards the instrument, still holding the ring and the lock of hair. It had been cut off, not pulled out by the roots; that almost gave him solace.

"Dawlish speaking."

"You'll have found it by now," the man said laconically. "Just sit back and do nothing, we want to talk to you. Wait for us, pal. You can still find what you want if you're patient. Okay?"

Dawlish said slowly, "Go and have a talk with Clay."

"We know about Clay," the man said; it would be easy to imagine that he was forcing back a laugh. "It was just too bad. It would be too bad if anything like that happened to the lady, wouldn't it? *Your* lady, pal. If Morgan comes to see you, slam the door in his face. See you."

The line went dead.

Dawlish stood with his back to the wall, and analysed the significance of those calls, the ring and the hair. They—say Kramer—wanted him to stay on at the Canyon, and hoped to frighten him into staying. Why didn't they want him to leave? Where did they expect him to go? Where was the obvious place for him to go?

After Clay. Where else? Kramer? No, they didn't know that he was on to Kramer.

Clay might have told them he'd talked of the redwoods and Highway 101, so they might think he would go there to find out more, but that was vague, Clay wasn't; Clay was the man to follow.

The telephone-bell rang again. Dawlish turned and looked at it. He could lean backwards and take off the receiver, but he didn't want more talk with the man with the laconic voice. It might be anyone—Morgan, remember, or Elliott. He leaned back.

"Dawlish speaking."

"It seems to me you must be a very busy man," drawled Sheriff Morgan. "I've tried to reach you twice, each time the line was busy. Have you found some friends?"

"Two," said Dawlish. "I think. One is named Elliott and the other is named Morgan." There was no lightness in his voice.

"Maybe you're right at that," Morgan answered; he took an age to utter a short sentence. "You've also made one enemy, or my thinking is even more crooked than usual. I know what happened to Clay. He's on his way out, the woman's driving him in that sky-blue Packard. They're heading West—maybe they told you."

"Why are you telling me?"

"I want you to know," said Morgan. Probably his eyes were screwed up in that smile which gave his face a thousand tiny lines. "He had his arm put in a sling at the hospital, and wouldn't say who did all that damage to him. It takes a powerful man to do that to a powerful man. Dawlish, I wouldn't object if you followed Clay. He'll be held up long enough at the exit from the Park to give you a chance to get close behind him. You know his car."

"And you'll know mine, when you bring up the rear."

"Why don't you just go ahead and do things instead of making so many guesses? You must think even more than I do. Take it from me, I want you to go. I've been told about the two telephone calls, and I've been thinking. The man who called you wants you to wait right here. Now why should he? and where would he expect you to go if you didn't wait?"

Dawlish said. "You tell me."

"You'd follow Clay, wouldn't you? There just isn't any other place you'd go. And if they want you to wait, I wanted you to follow Clay. I guess you don't have to, but——"

"I'll go," Dawlish said.

"That's fine. If you hear a police siren behind you, it won't be because of speeding," Morgan said. "Just pull in, the cop will have a message for you. Maybe you'll take a lot of convincing but there are some mighty big advantages in working with the police, friend. We'll see you don't take the wrong road. How soon can you start?"

"In twenty minutes."

"Make it fifteen. Anything you want to ask me, now I'm here?"

"Do the redwoods near Highway 101 mean anything to you?"

"Clay mention them?"

"Yes. Also a disused lumber-mill."

"That could be a stall. Right now it means just what it says, but when I've thought about it and maybe acted some, it might mean more. Be careful with Clay when you meet him again. Be even more careful of his wife."

"*Wife?*" echoed Dawlish.

"Well, that's how they registered," Morgan said dryly. "But what am I thinking of, wasting time talking? You'll get some messages on the way. And I hope you have some luck—all the luck you deserve." He paused. "What's this man Kramer?"

Dawlish told him briefly.

"Could be you've found something," Morgan said. "I didn't get your message until he'd gone. I've asked the police along all the highways leading out of here to report when they see his car, a red Ford. We'll catch up with him. Want him questioned?" There was almost a laugh in Morgan's voice.

"If I were a policeman I'd wait until I knew I could put him inside before I talked to him—or to Clay," Dawlish said. "So long."

CHAPTER XII

SLOW CHASE

THE sky blue of the Packard showed up for a hundred yards before Dawlish reached it. He slowed down. He was half a mile beyond Williams, with motor-courts, restaurants and garages on either side. This wasn't far from the Canyon, not so far as he expected Clay to be at his first stop. He drew near enough to see that the car was empty, then put his foot down; he was doing seventy as he passed the Packard, which was outside a restaurant, and kept seventy up for several minutes. He pulled in off the road just over the brow of a long, low hill, lit a cigarette, and walked to the top of the hill. He could see for miles. Cars were swooping towards him, some near, some a long way off; he could pick out the colours almost as far away as the skyline, the air was so clear.

There was nowhere to hide his car.

No one had appeared to shadow the Buick, but a dozen cars had passed it on the road. The sky-blue Packard hadn't put on any great speed; perhaps Clay was in too much pain to stand speed.

Dawlish saw it suddenly, just over the skyline. He turned back to the Buick and started off half a mile ahead. He touched seventy again. In places the road was straight for two or three miles, a fair width, with rough edges and barren land stretching out on either side, touched with the magic colours of early evening. There were few clouds.

At the end of a long straight stretch, Dawlish saw six cars in the driving-mirror but not the Packard. He slowed down and more cars passed him. The Packard came into sight and he put on another spurt. An hour, doing that, told him that the Packard was doing a steady fifty; most traffic on the road was doing at least seventy, only the huge silver-grey trucks were slower.

There wasn't much left of daylight; it was already after six o'clock, soon after seven it would begin to get dark, and there was no long, helpful dusk. In the darkness he would have to follow. He wasn't sure that the trouble he had taken was worth-while; was he fooling Clay? Should he try?

Once it was so dark that he could not tell the colours of the cars behind, he pulled off the road again, outside a hot-dog stand, near a garage. Only a faded-looking woman was at the stand, on the business side, and she looked at Dawlish without interest, stretched out her hand automatically for a wiener sizzling on a hot-plate. Cooked food made the heat seem worse.

"One please, and coffee," Dawlish said, and wiped his neck.

She nodded; the unfamiliar accent didn't raise a spark of interest, but coffee and the sausage between a long white roll were in Dawlish's hands almost as soon as he finished speaking; and his money was in hers. He turned his back on her and watched the road. Headlights drew near and flashed by; he had to be sure that he didn't miss the Packard. It was a long time coming, so long that he began to wonder whether it had stopped, or left the road, or even turned back. He could have been too clever, giving Clay a chance to double back—that was, if Clay didn't want to be followed.

The chase was much slower than he had expected; painfully slow. It gave him too much time to think about things which didn't help; too much time to fondle that lock of hair. He finished the hot-dog and coffee, and walked towards the side of the road, some way from the stand; he was no longer against its light. Headlights just missed him. He saw the Packard as it passed, and recognized Eloise at the wheel. He didn't notice Clay. He stared after the car and thought that he saw the back of a man's head through the rear window; perhaps Clay was taking it easy in the back.

Dawlish started off.

Now and again, he slackened speed to let the Packard get farther ahead, but he wouldn't let it go too far out of sight.

The lights of a small township showed ahead, bright and many-coloured. Advertisement signs for the motor-courts and the garages flamed a long time before he reached them. In the light of the approach to the village he could see the Packard, and it seemed to be going much more slowly than usual. It was—it stopped. As Dawlish passed, he saw Eloise stepping from the car outside a motor-court where a red neon sign flashed VACANCIES on and off. Dawlish pulled up some way along, hidden by other cars from Clay or anyone else who was watching. He strolled back. People were walking, talking, cars humming past, cars were parked outside the motor-courts, restaurants and soda fountains; there was plenty of life in spite of the heat. From outside a soda fountain where a juke-box was giving a rendering of 'Sweet Violets', he saw the girl come out of the motor-court, get into the car, and then drive into the court.

So they were going to stay the night.

A green sign above the red VACANCIES glowed PANCHO COURT.

Probably Clay hadn't been able to stand the journey; he might be in a worse way than Dawlish knew.

Dawlish walked back to the Buick. A few yards farther along the NAVAJO MOTEL offered vacancies. He went towards it and a brisk, elderly man in his shirt-sleeves came out of a small office.

"Can I help you?" His drawl was slower than Morgan's.

"Have you a room with a window overlooking the road?" asked Dawlish.

The man glanced up with sharp interest, but didn't ask questions. The neon lighting made him look as if he were made up for the footlights.

"Most folk want to get away from the road, I guess, but I've got just that. You want to come into the office? I'll get the keys."

The room was the first on the little court, with a double bed and the shower, an easy chair, all clean and comfortable. Dawlish paid four dollars and was given the key, and the man left him. Dawlish pulled the Buick up, took out one suitcase packed with what he wanted for the night, and sat down with a cigarette between his lips. He wished he knew why Clay and Eloise had stopped so early; it was almost as if they meant to give him a chance to catch up with them; that might mean they had taken it for granted that he would follow.

He wasn't hungry.

He went out, and a motor-cycle cop standing by the side of his machine said, "Hi!" He had a broad face and a broad grin, with big, wide-spaced teeth. He needed a shave, and sweat made the sides of his face wet; there were tiny beads of sweat on his nose. He wore a peaked cap, khaki shirt and trousers, and leather boots with leggings over bow-legs. There were hundreds like him, even though his eyes had a merrier smile than most.

"Hallo," said Dawlish, almost hopefully.

"You Mr. Dawlish?"

"Yes." Morgan had kept his word; and doubtless always would.

"I guess you want to know that the Packard's at the Pancho Court."

"I knew it was near. Fine. Thanks."

"You're welcome." The man looked into his face and grinned more expansively. "How do you like our little country, sir?"

"You can count me as a convert."

"What's that?"

"I like it a lot."

"Why, that's fine," said the cop enthusiastically. "That's what I like to hear, Mr. Dawlish. It's a mighty fine country, you can take it from me—there isn't any place like it in the world. You staying here long?"

"As long as I can."

"That's fine! Well, I'll be getting along." The cop grinned, straddled his machine, and turned expertly into the sluggish stream of traffic. As Dawlish watched him go he could hear the music from two or three juke-boxes; there was all noise and life. He went nearer the Pancho Court; the Packard was three huts in, there was a light at the window. It looked as if Clay and Eloise would settle for the night, and, what mattered most, also looked as if he could rely on getting a call when they moved off. He needed no telling that Morgan would do a good job.

He went back to his own court. If Kramer wanted to kidnap him he might try in a lot of places but he wouldn't try here; it was more likely to happen on the open road, farther on into the desert. He could forget worry about his own safety, but that was the only worry he could forget.

He had a meal of fried chicken and a sundae, sat drinking coffee and imagining the bright interest in Felicity's eyes when she had seen these gaily-lighted restaurants, the throbbing, pulsing vitality of the small townships. Felicity, Felicity. Into his mind's eye there came a photograph in a newspaper, of a woman, hanging.

He strolled past the Pancho Court. The light was out at the third window but the Packard was still there. It was after nine; Clay might make an early start and Dawlish had plenty of sleep to catch up, if he could get to sleep. He went back to the motel; a man and a woman two doors away called, "Howdy?" but didn't come across to talk when he answered. He went in, had a shower, and got into his pyjamas and into bed, relying on the police to call him if he weren't up when Clay made a move. It had been slow and unsatisfactory, and he was full of doubts.

Sleep didn't come easily, but it came.

It was still dark when knocking at the door woke him.

He opened his eyes and sleep drained out of him, leaving him flat and empty but alert. Had he been wrong? He lay on his back, and the knock came again. It was dark outside except for the neon lighting, so it might be any time before half past five.

"Coming." He got out of bed, took the small automatic out of his coat pocket, went to the door and opened it cautiously; there wasn't a thing he could take for granted, no certainty that this would be a policeman.

It was Eloise; the neon lighting shining on her red hair turned it into burnished, green-tinted copper. She stood close to the door, and as it opened she pushed it quickly. He let her come in, and closed the door as soon as she was inside; it was very dark except for the green glow through the window. She wasn't breathing heavily.

"So the boss let his nurse off for an hour," Dawlish said. "Think he would approve of this, beautiful?"

He kept his gun in his hand, by his side.

CHAPTER XIII

RED BEAUTY

ELOISE didn't answer, but turned her back on him; he could see her silhouette against the window. She stretched up and drew the curtains, turned to face him again, as he put on the light. It was so bright that it made him narrow his eyes; she closed hers. She wore a yellow linen dress, and while it wasn't too small for her, it stretched in places to give the emphasis she would always want her clothes to give. She was ripe; she was beautiful; and she had been fooling someone in the shack at the Canyon.

If she were agitated, she hid it by a calmness which could

be forced. He went to the table by the side of the bed and picked up his cigarettes. They lit up.

"Thank you."

"You're welcome."

"I expected you to come and see Clay."

"I could think of a lot of men who are under the daisies because they did what the other man expected." Dawlish went across to the easy chair and sat down, waved to the bed, and went on, "Make yourself comfortable."

"I'm comfortable. You could do what you like with Clay right now."

"That so?"

"I'm telling you." Her voice wasn't exactly clipped, but she seemed to be making sure that every word counted; it wasn't the eager outpourings as in the shack before Trig Clay had arrived and she had shown that she could be afraid of him. "He had a lot of pain in that shoulder and his ribs—he cracked two ribs, also. So I gave him a shot."

"The kindly nurse," Dawlish murmured. "Do you carry a hypo and morphia around with you?"

"Trig does. There are a lot of ways of getting hurt," Eloise said carefully. "He'll be as still as a dead man for the next two or three hours."

"If you go on like this," Dawlish taunted, "I shall begin to think that you're not so fond of Clay as you pretended to be."

It was some time before she answered; then it was obliquely.

"Usually he doesn't talk to me. Not about business. But there isn't so much he can do for himself right now and he had to confide in me this time. He reckoned you would follow. Somewhere on the road he's going to snatch you."

"He was going to kill," said Dawlish lightly.

"He wants you to talk first."

"Clay does?" Dawlish made himself sound surprised.

"He said so."

"What does he want?"

"He didn't tell me everything."

"That's too bad. Did he tell you to come and talk to me, beautiful, or did you think all this up in your own pretty mind?"

"He's unconscious," Eloise said, carefully. "If I had the nerve, I would cut his throat myself."

That sounded worse than it would have done had she shouted,

had she been in a rage. The quietness of her voice hinted at a slow-burning hatred, began to convince Dawlish that she was here because she wanted to put Clay on the losing side.

Dawlish said, "What time is it?" He glanced round at his watch, on the bedside-table, but she answered:

"It's some time after one."

"And he's alone? You weren't followed? He doesn't have a bodyguard?"

"If he has, I wouldn't know," she said. "You'll never find him so easy to fix as he is now." She held out her hand; a key was in it.

Dawlish said: "If you're lying, my lovely, I'll have Clay and you to deal with later." He took the key, then the hanger with his clothes on and went into the shower, drew the curtain, and dressed with difficulty in the tiny space. Eloise was still there when he came out, buttoning up his shirt. He sat on the edge of the bed and put on his shoes.

"If you feel like it, you could climb out of the window," Dawlish said. He took the key and went out, closed and locked the door, and walked away. He didn't go far. The night air was cool compared with the heat of the day and the warmth of the evening, and he needed something to cool him. Few people were about, but the signs still blazed and cars still passed, their headlights full on. Dawlish waited two or three minutes and then went softly back towards his room. He approached the window from one side. There was a gap in the curtains, and he peered through.

Eloise lay on the bed, knees drawn, up, head on his pillow, cigarette between her lips. She looked relaxed, comfortable, prepared to wait for a long time.

Dawlish moved away.

If Clay had schemed this, he would be awake, not unconscious; and when Dawlish got in, he would probably learn whether 'Trig' had anything to do with trigger. But Clay with a badly bruised arm and plenty of other bruises even if he had no cracked ribs, wouldn't plan to deal with him alone. There would be others.

Dawlish drew level with Pancho Court, on the opposite side of the road. The light still burned in the office, but all the huts were in darkness. Dawlish looked about him, and saw no one, went across the road, but could not be sure that no one was lurking in the darkness. He went to the third hut, and listened; there was no sound.

He put the key in, turned, waited, and went in; there was only darkness.

He switched on his torch. The pale beam shone on the big double bed and on Clay, lying on his back, eyes closed; he hardly seemed to be breathing. Dawlish went closer, shone the torch right into his eyes; the lids didn't flicker. He raised one eyelid; the pupil was a pin-point, and hardly visible—just as it would be if he'd had a morphia injection. Dawlish doubted if he would come out of this sleep for several hours. He looked into the shower; no one was there, nothing suggested that anyone was watching or that Eloise had lied. He searched the pockets of Clay's clothes; his baggage, and a case that belonged to Eloise. Nothing was helpful.

He went out.

. . . . .

Eloise was lying on the bed, head snuggled deeper into the pillows, and she wasn't smoking. She looked as if she would have fallen asleep had Dawlish been any longer. She didn't open her eyes wide, which was a pity, because they were beautiful eyes. Dawlish stood at the foot of the bed, looking down at her, twisting the key of Clay's room about his finger.

"What makes you hate Clay like that?"

He thought that she was going to refuse to answer, but when he was about to speak again, she said in the same quiet voice:

"He's a killer. That's none of my business. He killed a man who was my business. It wouldn't occur to Clay that it would matter to me who I slept with, but it matters." Her fine lips curved sardonically. "I like to cross some off my list."

"So he murdered your boy-friend."

"That's right," Eloise said. "There isn't anyone more dangerous than Trig Clay. He'll get you if you give him a chance. I've given you a chance to get him. What are you going to make of it?"

Dawlish tossed the key on to the bed by her side.

"Nothing," he said. "Yet. Clay's just as you left him. You go back. This didn't happen. I don't want Clay just yet, but I shall want him later, and I might be able to use help then."

She sat up, slowly, and there was searing contempt in her eyes, the twist of her lips was ugly.

"You goddamned fool, there will never be another chance like this! I give it to you and you throw it away. I thought you were good. I saw the way you smashed him up and I thought I'd found someone who would take any chance to finish him off. You could take him away, do anything with him, you've thrown the chance in my teeth." She got off the bed slowly, her voice quivered as if with anger; she looked as if she would like to spit at him, and her green eyes held a blazing light. "I ought to have known no limey had real guts."

Dawlish smiled faintly.

"Yes, you ought. Did Clay tell you what I want from him?"

"You'll never have a better chance to get what you want."

"So he didn't."

Something in his expression silenced her, dulled her anger. "No."

Dawlish put his left hand into his pocket and took out the hair with the wedding-ring in the middle. The platinum gleamed dully, and the grey strands showed up in the lamplight. He held it for several seconds, until Eloise had stopped looking at it, and was staring at him, wondering, questioning.

"My wife's hair. My wife's wedding-ring. I think Clay knows where she is. I'm going to find out. I could kill him or I could smash him up more than he's smashed up now, but I don't think I could make him talk if he didn't want to talk. He may be a killer but he isn't yellow." He paused. "Is he?"

"I'm beginning to see it your way," Eloise whispered, and came closer, as if she were anxious to get a better look at the ring. Dawlish closed his hand round it, and slipped it back into his pocket. "But that's exactly what he wants you to do. He'll have a trap ready to spring the moment he thinks you'll fall for it."

"I was halfway to guessing," Dawlish said. "Thanks all the same, beautiful. Have you ever heard of a man named Kramer?"

That didn't startle her, didn't seem an unlikely question; she simply said, "Yes."

"Is he a friend of Clay's?"

"He works for Clay."

"Well, well," said Dawlish. "And who does Clay work for?"

"It wouldn't be like Clay," she said. "He's the big shot. He isn't one to take orders from anyone. But I can tell you this—

Kramer doesn't know Clay's the boss. Kramer thinks he's just another legman."

If she were right, then Clay was the man who mattered; but even if she thought he were, Clay might have fooled her. Vanity in the man could be so deep that it would influence everything he did, even his way of thinking.

"That's fine," Dawlish said. "Go back to Clay and forget all this, Eloise. There'll come a time when we can take things up where we left off. Perhaps we could have another little chat, some time when you've persuaded Clay to tell you more than he has; perhaps even when he's told you where my wife is."

She shook her head slowly.

"I don't think he'll ever do that," she said. "He was so sick he wasn't himself. In the morning he'll be back to normal. I've seen him as bad as this before. Once he had a bullet in his chest and most men would have folded up, but in a few days he was just Trig Clay. There may not be another chance. If there is, I'll take it—so long as I can keep in the clear myself."

Dawlish nodded. Eloise went to the door. He stopped her from opening it, went outside himself, leaving her in the room. He closed the door and walked round, crossed the road, made as sure as he could be sure that they weren't being watched. Then he went back for her. Before they parted she caught his hand and squeezed, and seemed reluctant to let go. Then she walked away, keeping this side of the road, and the yellow of her dress and the beauty of her hair gradually dimmed, until he lost sight of her.

He turned back to the room.

A man said, "Having visitors, Mr. Dawlish?"

CHAPTER XIV

THE GAMBLER

DAWLISH spun on his heel. The man came out from behind the office, with the lighted door open behind him. It was the traffic cop, and his grin was huge. Dawlish matched it, but his heart thumped. The cop didn't matter; the fact that others could have been watching from there, perhaps from another room, mattered a great deal.

"Wishing you were me?" he asked mildly.

"I sure agree she's got everything." The cop took out cigarettes and offered them. "I've been told that you know you have to watch her as closely as you'd watch a snake." He lit his cigarette, still smiling.

"That's how closely I'm watching," Dawlish said.

"So long as you are."

"Anyone keeping an eye on Clay?"

"You bet."

"Seen anyone else about?" asked Dawlish. "Clay has friends who might be keeping a careful eye on him."

"I guess I haven't seen anyone around; it looks as if Clay's playing this solo. He plays most things solo."

"You know him so well?"

The cop chuckled. "We get to know, Mr. Dawlish. Clay's quite something in Las Vegas. There are still plenty of big gamblers, and you can take it from me he gambles high. You're likely to find him in the Big Stakes saloon, and if he isn't there, in the hotel close by—the Gamblers."

Why hadn't Morgan known something about this? Or if he knew, why hadn't he said so?

"Is that general knowledge?"

"We get to know things," the cop said confidently.

. . . . . .

He was awake by eight o'clock, bathed and breakfasted by a quarter to nine, on the road in the wake of the blue Packard by twenty past ten. Clay was in the back. He looked less rested than comatose, but this morning Eloise kept her foot down and the road was made for speed.

They didn't stop in the green beauty of Boulder City, slowed down only as they went across the dam, with sightseers crowding the walls, put on speed again now that they were in Nevada. They didn't stop for food. They reached Las Vegas at half past three, and the city lay beneath a sweltering sun; Dawlish had never felt so hot.

When he passed the Packard outside the Gamblers Hotel, Eloise was helping Clay from the car and looking as cool as if it were midnight.

Clay didn't glance at Dawlish until the girl said something. Then he glanced round. Eloise had told him—why not? Eloise knew that if Dawlish were prepared to pass so closely, he didn't mind Clay knowing he was on the trail.

He didn't mind.

• • • • •

Dawlish put up at a motor-court close to the centre of the city, had a shower, changed his shirt, and went out. There was everything in the world to make him heedless of new scenes and new places; but he began to look about him with quickening interest in the things he saw.

The gaming saloons were side by side in the main streets and those leading off it. Neon signs competed garishly with full daylight. Hot sweaty crowds jostled on the sidewalk and inside the saloons. Money-changers with stacks of silver dollars in front of them switched these for dollar bills without showing the slightest interest.

Dawlish turned into the Big Stake saloon; it seemed vaster than any of the others. Lights blazed, and it was fiercely hot. Every face seemed lined with sweat but the heat took nothing of the intentness out of the eyes of the gamblers or the watchfulness of the croupiers, the money-changers, the men who held the banks. At the entrance, slot machines were being pulled, pushed, shaken; now and again the jackpot spilled out. Men sat at small tables, playing poker, as well as a dozen games Dawlish didn't know. People stood and watched, hungrily, greedily. There was noise all the time, yet the quiet voices of the men in command came through the babble.

Dawlish went towards the biggest crowd; the game was roulette. The croupiers sat jostled by the people who pressed forward. Chips dropped on to the green baize, were pushed into position; the ball went spinning into the wheel and the wheel turned.

"Nine wins."

Chips vanished from some, appeared in front of others. Most went to someone Dawlish could not see. He shifted his position.

Clay, arm in a sling, sat there. His left hand was on the table, close to a big heap of chips. He looked at nothing, or appeared to look at nothing but the wheel and the table. Dawlish made his way round; Clay didn't glance up. After ten minutes a red-faced man, who looked as if he had been in the sun for the first time this year, groaned as his last chips went and got up. Dawlish elbowed another man out of the way and took the vacant place, opposite Clay. He couldn't gamble high, but took this as a challenge to come into the open; Clay had seen him. A hundred dollars was more than a hundred to him, to the friends who had financed the search, but a hundred dollars might be worth losing; even if he lost. He kept a poker-face, glanced occasionally at Clay but at no one else.

Eloise wasn't there.

Dawlish divided his chips into four and put one pile on to eleven. He went down. He put the next on eleven and went down again. Clay won once. Dawlish, attracting attention with his unfamiliar voice, repeated his number. Clay put a big pile on twelve, and that wasn't an accident. He didn't look up.

The droning voice of the banker came.

"Eleven wins."

Dawlish collected chips worth nine hundred dollars. He put a hundred on eleven five times; the fifth turned up. He kept poker-faced as the winnings were pushed towards him; three thousand six hundred dollars.

A wise man would stop now.

He put a hundred on eleven and lost six times running; Clay stuck to twelve, and didn't win once. He was cleaned out unless he bought more chips. He didn't, but stood up. Dawlish collected his chips, watched by envious crowds, changed them into bills; over three thousand dollars. Clay had lost at least a thousand.

Dawlish caught up with him by the door.

"That's how it's going to happen to you from now on." He went off before the crowd had realized he had talked to Clay. Clay followed. They met in the street, without speaking, and then turned right towards the Gamblers. Clay walked awkwardly; undoubtedly his ribs hurt.

Outside the hotel, Clay said: "I told you I was through. One day I'll get you, if I have to come to England to do it, but right now you've someone else to worry about." He looked into Dawlish's eyes, his own without any expression, turned and limped into the hotel. Dawlish walked on. So Clay still wanted to make him believe that he had withdrawn, that the fight was really with Kramer; which meant that Clay remained anxious to keep in the background. Kramer didn't know him as the boss; Dawlish couldn't have been sure, but for Eloise. Could he be sure now?

He went back to his motor-court, was glad to step into the coolness of one big room, took off his tie and wrapped it absently round his hand, and then saw the letter. It stood on the one grip he had brought in, and his name was written on it in purple ink; the writing was big and careless. He hesitated before opening it.

I think she's at a cattle ranch, the One Shoe. Don't tell anyone you're being followed.

• • • • •

There was no way of being sure that the note was from Eloise; Dawlish could only guess that it was her writing; she would probably write like that. In the first flush of a strange, gripping excitement, all he could think about was the first sentence, the possibility that he was near Felicity.

He made himself think; made himself remember that Eloise could have fooled him, and that this might be no more than part of the trick to get possession of him.

The note had one thing right; he was being followed.

He went to the window and looked out. At the far end of the big court, with twenty or more huts on either side, stood two men; they had followed him from the Gamblers. If they'd followed, they would probably have the motor-court watched, which meant that Eloise would have been seen had she come here herself.

She wouldn't have done that; if Clay were so well known in Las Vegas, she would be.

The One Shoe cattle ranch meant nothing but it should be easy to find out plenty about it. There was no hurry for the next hour or two; getting rid of the men who followed him came first. To do that, he would have to make himself familiar with the lay-out of the town. He took the car and drove around. The two men followed in a black sedan.

Hardly a moment passed without him seeing the first sentence in the note: *I think she's at a cattle ranch, the One Shoe.* Now that he had absorbed that, the argument that there was no hurry vanished; everything was urgent. The danger was that he would make a fatal mistake by hurrying. When he inquired about the One Shoe it must be when he wasn't being watched.

He parked the car in town; the two men parked theirs nearby and followed him on foot. He turned into a restaurant; they also turned in. He sat at an otherwise empty table, and they sat two tables away. The waiter came up casually, put a menu in front of him, then a glass of iced water, and went off. Dawlish studied the menu. When the waiter came back he ordered a T-bone steak and French fried potatoes; next time the waiter slipped up and gave him a second folded paper serviette. He didn't think anything of it, until the meal arrived and the waiter bent close to him as he put it down and said:

"Second serviette," so softly that Dawlish wasn't sure what he had said until he had gone.

Dawlish started to eat, then opened the serviette cautiously. There was a sheet of paper pinned to it, and the message was right to the point.

Get rid of the two legmen and come to 15, *Sunrise Auto Court.*

Sketched in place of a signature was a Sheriff's badge.

CHAPTER XV

ONE SHOE RANCH

IT WAS a big room and there were two other men in it. Morgan introduced them as Fritz Weiner and Larry Grey. All over the world they would have looked like plain-clothes policemen. They were obviously here with a watching brief. Morgan did the talking, and the change of air from Arizona to Nevada seemed to have quickened the pace of his speech.

"The first thing is to congratulate you, I guess," he said dryly. "On being alive. The second is to tell you not to try to do a thing to Clay in this township. Clay has too many friends. I'm beginning to think maybe I was wrong about him. He's taken a suite at the Gamblers for three weeks."

"Perhaps he feels like a rest," Dawlish said dryly. There was a lot that Morgan didn't know, and in return for this kind of help, Morgan deserved to. "Are you in the right mood for listening?"

"Try me." Morgan took out a cigar, unwrapped and lit it. "Why don't we have a drink, Fritz, no one told me Nevada was a dry state?"

Fritz, the heavier of the two policemen, mixed drinks; someone had been thoughtful enough to provide Scotch but there was no soda.

"Have you found Kramer?" Dawlish asked.

"There's a guy named Kramer known to work for Clay but what work he does no one can guess," Morgan said. "We didn't pick up his car. He's known in Las Vegas but hasn't been seen here for a week or more. One thing will interest you. Every time Clay went to the Canyon, Kramer was there."

Dawlish said, "Was he, then?"

"What do you know?" Morgan asked him.

He talked while the drinks were being mixed, didn't touch his until he had finished, with three pairs of eyes on him all the time.

Larry Grey, shorter than Fritz by inches and smaller round the waist by half a foot, broke the silence.

"One Shoe's one hell of a place, twenty miles along a dirt road that leads nowhere else. If they want to snatch anyone, that's the place to fix it." He had the dreary voice of a natural pessimist.

"There's one thing we could forget," Morgan said, looking at the half-inch of ash on his cigar. "If Clay's wife is on the level, no one will expect Dawlish to head for One Shoe, and right now no one knows which way he's heading. You've got yourself a different car," he added casually. "It seemed to us that Buick could be recognized too easily. From now on you'll drive a Mercury."

Dawlish said: "That suits me. Thanks."

Larry Grey had been ruminating, and gave his opinion gloomily.

"Maybe she hates Clay's guts. Maybe she doesn't. Clay's staked her with plenty. He picked her up when Hollywood threw her down, even the clip-joints wouldn't let her work, and if she throws Clay over, she'll throw plenty with it."

"Know anything about this man she was screwy about and Clay killed?"

Larry and Fritz shook their heads.

"We wouldn't, if it didn't happen here," Larry said. "And it didn't."

"You feel like taking a chance at One Shoe?" Morgan asked Dawlish. "At dawn, maybe, not by night—lights shine too far at night."

"It may be the oldest trap in the world," Dawlish said, "but if there's half a chance my wife is there, I'm going."

Larry looked more gloomy than ever.

"You boys could have some men around," Morgan said, "just to make sure our friend from England doesn't get hurt too badly. Couldn't you, Fritz?"

"Oh, sure."

"Let's do that," Morgan said, "Even if it's less than the half-chance Dawlish hopes it is. If you leave your court at sun-up, Dawlish, that will be the best time. Not the court you've booked in, you can get yourself another. Not this one, either, Clay might be told that I'm around. It isn't likely I'll be recognized, but it could happen."

• • • • •

Dawlish had learned a great deal about One Shoe ranch. It was a small cattle outfit in country where one steer grazed to ten acres; country one could drive through without seeing a steer from morning until night. It was run by an old man named Rinker and two hired men; the hired men changed season by season, sometimes in the season. Part of the time, Rinker lived there alone. It was in a shallow valley, where the heat collected during the day and stayed by night, so that it was always several degrees hotter than Las Vegas. There was some water. The road to it fed several other ranches and a small mine, but these were reached by dirt roads which branched off; for the last ten miles the road was little more than a trail made by cattle, horses and Rinker's 1930 Ford. Some of his hired men had cars also.

It was a forgotten ranch in a forgotten valley. When Rinker died, no one was ever likely to take it over; it would go derelict, become another ghost outfit.

In a grey Mercury, Dawlish drove along the dirt road until he came to a sign which pointed three ways and the way ahead was: *One Shoe*. Nothing and no one was in sight. Although dawn was only half an hour past, it was hot with the kind of heat that closed round one and crept up from all sides, from above and from beneath. The sun, just above the horizon, already seemed hot. The sky was a miracle of colour and cloud;

breath-taking. Even in his mood he felt the effect of its awesome beauty. The soil was mostly sand, with tufts of grass and here and there mesquite which grew little more than knee high, and an occasional yucca plant, other cacti-like plants he didn't recognize.

The only breaks in the yellow-grey monotony of the land were rock outcrops, and there weren't many. The biggest were not large enough to hide Dawlish or a quarter of his car. He drove slowly, making a trail of dust behind him, and guessed that if men waited for him at One Shoe, he would be seen before he could see the ranch building or the outhouses. He kept licking his warm sticky lips, which were coated with fine alkali dust. He wore a shirt which would probably betray to the practised eye that he had the gun in the shoulder holster; his coat was draped over the seat next to him.

He just drove on and it seemed for ever, but at last he saw the ranch-house, through eyes narrowed against the heat and the morning glare and the dust. It wasn't far away. He saw the old car, no one could mistake the T-model Ford, standing under a roof—a kind of shed with no sides. He saw chickens scratching, and two cows roaming loose, three horses in a corral; they were the only signs of life. He didn't see a modern car, but one might be hidden round the other side of the ranch-house. The highest thing of all was the watermill, its sails turning sluggishly. It was electrically operated, drawing water from two hundred feet below the earth.

The house, of frame, hadn't been painted for years and already looked derelict. No one stirred.

Dawlish drove past the house and round it; there was no sign of another car. He drew up outside the front door and approached it. Three wooden steps led up to a wooden verandah, and some of the boards were split. Curtains hung at the windows, a concession to tradition; the house couldn't be overlooked. Wilting wistaria tried to climb one of the walls but finished short of the wide iron guttering. The air was so hot it was like breathing through cotton wool.

Dawlish banged on the door.

There was no answer.

He turned and looked behind him, and saw no sign of another car, nothing to suggest that the police had followed. They had probably come ahead of him, but if they had, where could they hide?

He must forget the police, and remind himself that Felicity might have been here. It wasn't even half a chance, but it was enough to make him grit his teeth. She might *be* here.

He banged on the door again, and then footsteps sounded. He drew back so that he was on the edge of the top step. The door began to open, and creaked loudly; then he saw an old man, more wizened and more wrinkled than Sheriff Morgan, almost as thin, who looked as if the heat had dried out his blood. He had eyes which had once been blue, but the colour had been drawn out of them.

"Mr. Rinker?" Dawlish almost choked.

"I'm Rinker." The voice was as tired as the man looked. He wore an old faded shirt and old faded trousers, but his feet were bare, his toe-nails broken. "You want me?" Slowly, he opened the door wider. He made Dawlish think that he would never be surprised at anything, would never make a protest, had lost any spirit the good Lord had put into him. "You from Kramer?"

It came just like that.

"Yes," Dawlish said. "I'm from Kramer." He couldn't get inside quickly enough, and he almost forgot the heat. He kept his right hand in his pocket round the automatic, and a coating of sweat was between his palm and the butt of the gun. "He wants me to talk to the woman."

"That so?" asked Rinker, in a cracked voice. "If it's okay by Kramer I guess it's okay by me."

Nothing in the way of a denial, just a calm acceptance of the fact that a woman was here, a woman Kramer knew about. Dawlish felt as if his chest were going to burst. He stood in a big, dark, hot room, where a fan turned and caused a breeze which only stirred the stifling air.

"Where is she?"

"Take your time, mister, take your time." Rinker went shuffling across the bare boards. Two hand-woven woollen Indian rugs were the only covering, there was a bare-topped table, and spindly chairs including two rockers. "Just take your time," he repeated, and led the way to a door in one corner; there were two doors, one wide open and showing a bedroom, the other was locked and the big black iron key stuck out of the keyhole. Dawlish held himself rigid, to stop from snatching at it. The old man's knuckly hands seemed to lack the strength to turn the key. It grated; it turned. Slowly, Rinker put his fingers round the wooden handle. Dawlish began to tremble; and then he could wait no longer. He thrust forward, sent the door crashing back, strode into a room filled with daylight dimmed by a blind.

Sitting in a chair, bound to it by the wrists and ankles, was Eloise.

CHAPTER XVI

KRAMER

DAWLISH stopped moving; a brick wall couldn't have pulled him up more brutally. The blood seemed to drain out of him, taking away that wild hope. He swayed as he looked into Eloise's great eyes. He saw but didn't comprehend; her expression meant nothing, the cord which tied her meant nothing, the fact that her shirt was torn at the shoulders and the flesh beneath was cut and bruised meant nothing.

"Okay, Pop," a man said.

Dawlish didn't even look round, and didn't realize that he had heard the voice before, near the Big Rock at the Canyon's rim. He was knocked stupid, with the shock of disappointment—because he had told himself that there was no hope until the old man had spoken, when he had become sure that it was the end of the chase.

"Just put your hands high, Dawlish," the man said.

Dawlish didn't move his hands—not even the one in his pocket. There was silence. In the silence, his mind began to work again, but it was too late. A blow across the head made him reel sideways. He knew that a man leapt, pushed and sent him crashing. He felt hands snatching at his pockets and his shirt; when the man backed away, he was carrying the automatic and the revolver; there had been no need to ask Morgan for that shoulder holster.

"Now you two can have fun," the man said.

Dawlish was beginning to see. The door closed on the man, the key turned in the lock. Voices outside were low-pitched, then they faded. A man walked away, another shuffled. Dawlish picked himself up, slowly, awkwardly, and pressed a hand against his head; it hurt, but not with a desperate pain. He put a hand on the panel of a single bed, leaned heavily, moved round and sat down.

"For cripe's sake don't look like that," Eloise said hoarsely. "Don't look like that."

He was looking at her, but until she spoke had hardly realized that she was still there. He closed his eyes. When he opened them again the shock was still on him, but he could think, could understand how easily he had been fooled. He was even able to remind himself that Morgan had planned to get him out of any trouble he walked into.

"Clay found out," Eloise said, and her voice seemed to have lost everything. "He——"

"Keep quiet," Dawlish begged. "Just keep quiet for a while longer."

"Clay found out," she repeated, and stopped.

Dawlish looked slowly round the room. It was just a bedroom, with a table and a bowl and jug on it, the bed, two chairs, one of them with Eloise tied to it, mats by the side of the bed, a wardrobe of once polished pine with the door standing open. Something hanging up made him stare. He got up steadily, and went across to it, knowing that the woman watched every movement he made. He opened the door further; women's clothes hung inside, just a light-weight great-coat and a sundress. The coat wasn't familiar; the splash of red and yellow flowers on the cream linen of the dress was; he had been with Felicity when she had bought it in Paris.

He took it down, slowly, and crumpled it up in his right hand. When his grip slackened all effect of the shock had gone, he was himself again. His voice was peculiarly soft.

"Was she here when you arrived?"

"No one else was here." Eloise couldn't look away from the dress. "Is—is that——"

"Yes. What happened to you?"

"Clay found out. I don't know how he found out, but he came into the apartment and—and beat me up. Kramer—Kramer was there. He just grinned. I thought Clay was going to kill me. He—he knew about me coming to you last night. He *knew*. He made me tell him I'd sent you that note."

"So you sent that first?"

"Yes, he . . ." She seemed to find breathing difficult, as if she were choking. "He'd told me about this place. I'd never known him talk so much. I thought he was still light-headed.

Talked about your wife. Said you'd fall into any trap to find her. I thought it was safe to—to let you know."

"How did you find out where I was?"

"Men were watching you, and told him. I was there. It seemed so easy, so safe. Then he just went mad. Look . . ." she choked, "look at my arms, my——"

She broke off.

Dawlish went nearer. Her shirt was torn so badly that the straps and top of her brassière showed through; so did the weals, and there was blood. It hadn't happened long ago. He touched the cords, but there was more than cords; chains held her fast to the chair, and were padlocked. There was nothing he could do to help her, except let her talk while he looked round the room. The door as a door didn't matter, he could break that down in minutes; or smash the window. But how many men were here?

She told him that she had been brought from Las Vegas just before dawn, and been here for less than an hour when he had arrived.

"Is Clay coming?"

"I don't know what he's aiming to do."

"Did he—mention my wife? The second time?" Now Dawlish turned and looked at Eloise, and thought of nothing else.

"No." She was nearly sobbing. "No, he didn't. I—I think he'll kill us. Can't you . . ." She didn't even finish asking him whether he could do anything; it was as if she were sure that he couldn't. He turned away from her, clamping down on his thought. Then he heard an engine start up, and it didn't sound like a car engine; it roared like an aeroplane. He felt the room shake. He went to the window but the shutters prevented him from seeing out. Mosquitoes and flies hummed against the wire mesh frame outside. The roaring of the engine grew louder.

The roaring engine was on the ground, and there had been no runway laid out. He couldn't imagine an aeroplane taking off on this ground, ankle deep in sandy soil. He turned towards Eloise but before he spoke the door opened and the key hadn't grated in the lock.

A small man, the man who had taken his guns, covered him with one. A second stood behind him.

"Kramer!" Eloise burst out. "Let me out of here! You know what he'll do to me, you know."

Kramer hadn't a Stetson to hide his face or a scarf to conceal his mouth and chin. He was just any little man with a smooth sallow, complexion and dark hair which shone with grease, and a small mouth. He gave a sneering grin, the kind of grin that would come naturally to a sadist.

"Sure I know," he said. "You'll burn." He went to her, and bound her wrists to the chair with cord, took off the padlock; and all the time she screamed in terror.

"You can come out, Dawlish," Kramer said.

The engine was still roaring, but did not sound so loud, and the floor didn't shake.

"Come out and hurry," Kramer said, "or you'll burn too." He kept his distance, and in spite of the grin and the gloating in his voice, he was wary; perhaps he had been told how far Dawlish could jump. "I don't want to have to tell you again."

Dawlish said thinly. "What's this about burning?"

"It ain't much of an outfit," said Kramer. "It's time it was burned down. The old man's been paid plenty. Just step forward."

"Let me go!" Eloise screamed. She started to struggle against her bonds, to try to kick; her mouth was wide open and terror blazed in her eyes. "Let me get out of here!"

Dawlish said, "Let her loose."

"So you can still give orders," Kramer sneered. "Okay, Mick." He stepped aside but covered Dawlish with the gun. The other man moved out of sight for a moment, came back holding a long pole. He was near enough to use it as a weapon; his forearms looked like a mass of twisted cords as he raised it. Dawlish backed away. He didn't expect the pole to be thrust forward like a spear. It caught him in the stomach and the wind was driven out of him, pain streaked through his body. A man rushed, Dawlish felt hands grab at his; then something cool touched his wrists. His hands were handcuffed behind him, and a man who scarcely reached his shoulder pushed him forward. Kramer was just ahead all the time, covering him; they couldn't have been more wary of a mad bull.

Eloise went on screaming a gibberish which screeched against Dawlish's ears, brought him near madness, but he was helpless as they pushed him into the big room. A man he hadn't seen before was coming in, carrying a green can with one word stencilled on it in white: GAS. Here, that meant petrol. The man began to splash petrol round the room, and the smell was stifling.

Eloise's voice was one long, piercing scream.

Dawlish jumped round, but he hadn't a chance. The man with the pole thrust it forward, Dawlish ran into it and pitched headlong. He felt a blow on the head and his skull seemed to split; with the second blow it split, and blackness spilled into the crack.

. . . . .

Dawlish came round in the air. The droning of an engine added to the throbbing pain in his ears, to a screaming that wasn't there. He was leaning forward with his arms still fast behind him, his head jammed against the ceiling of a cabin or cockpit. The fierce sunlight struck at his eyes and he didn't want to open them; the droning engine seemed to screech and all he could see was Eloise with her mouth wide open and the terrified scream coming out.

He opened his eyes and saw the desert stretching out below him. He was aware of shadows, moving swiftly over him all the time. He looked up. The blades of a helicopter turned swiftly above his head.

The pilot was in front of him, but out of reach. He didn't know whether anyone else was behind him, and couldn't twist his head round in order to see. He looked below again, and saw tiny dots moving, like toy cars crawling. He watched them, and saw that there were four, each with a cloud of dust behind it. Then he saw something else ahead of the cars, a yellow mass with darker dust at the top of it, turning into a cloud.

Dust?

Smoke.

The ranch-house was blazing, and the cars seemed to be converging on to it, each engine screaming, screaming—and the screams were coming from a woman's mouth, lips stretched horribly over her white teeth.

Kramer spoke from behind Dawlish.

"That's how we do things, Limey. Too bad you didn't have time to say good-bye to Eloise."

. . . . .

Through the heat and the dull pain Dawlish fought for the sanity of calmness, and a measure came. Before the helicopter landed the screams from that distorted mouth were fading and so was the mental image of Eloise. He could see the sun-dress and accept it as evidence that Felicity had been at One Shoe ranch, not as fuel to feed his fear. He knew that the four toy cars had been police cars, even accepted hope that the police would reach the ranch before Eloise was burned alive.

He knew now how desperately anxious these men were to keep him alive; it could only be to make him name whoever had sent him. Was that why they had fed him with hope that Felicity was not dead?

When the helicopter had lifted him off the desert it had carried him out of the reach of the police. Morgan would try to trace him, but anyone who could plan and execute such a move would be confident of side-tracking the police. From now on, it was his fight; the way he had seen it first. In the new, flat calmness it would be easy to tell himself that he hadn't a chance, and fatal to believe it.

Kramer hadn't spoken again.

They had been in the air for at least an hour, and Dawlish had seen no houses, no signs of life, only occasional outcrops of rock and here and there the smooth bed of a river, a dry arroyo with the sun-baked mud in it cracked and lined like Morgan's face. The clouds had gone, the sky was pale blue. Ahead, he saw broken hills and beyond them higher ground with dark red rocks. Soon they were flying over this and looking down he could see the twisting shape of a small canyon, which from here looked deep and in places shadowy. A river with a ribbon of water ran through the main gorge and patches of cottonwoods, pale green against the reddy-yellow rock and the yellow sand, looked cool and shady.

They were losing height.

He searched the land around the Canyon and the Canyon itself for buildings, but saw none until they were only a few hundred feet above the ground. In a clearing among a cotton-wood copse was an L-shaped house, with outbuildings and fences, corrals where horses idled. A few hundred yards from the house the wall of the Canyon rose sheer.

Two men came out of the shade of the cottonwoods and looked up; a third came out of the house. Dawlish was near enough to see him walking down the steps but could not tell whether it was Clay; he couldn't be sure that Clay would be here. He wasn't sure that Felicity was here but he could hope.

Kramer prodded him in the back.

"You do what we tell you to do, Limey."

Dawlish didn't speak. The ground seemed to come up and meet them, he was prepared for a jolt but there was none. He was too stiff to move. Two of the men from the house came up, half-pulled and half-pushed him out, but he couldn't stand upright; so they let him fall, and spoke among themselves as if he didn't exist, until Kramer looked down at him and said:

"Don't take any chances with him, he can do as much damage as a mad elephant."

"He won't do any damage," another man said casually. "He talked?"

"No one's tried to make him yet."

"We going to soften him up?" It was less a question than a hope.

"Sure, and we're going to hurry."

"I know a way," the man from the house said. Dawlish couldn't see his face but could imagine his grin. "I know plenty of ways." the voice held brutish laughter. "He won't hold out for long."

The voices were calm and matter-of-fact, and because of that, more frightening. With his arms behind his back and the steel of the handcuffs biting into his wrists, Dawlish couldn't move. He strained against the steel and knew that there was no hope of breaking it, trying would only cause more pain. There was enough pain. It came partly from the burning sun, for where he lay there was no shade. He could see the glint of the river as it wound its way through the Canyon, but that gave only an illusion of coolness. Not fifty feet away from him the shadow beneath the cottonwoods was almost black and offered blessed sanctuary, but fifty feet was as far as fifty miles.

"You could use a drink, I guess," the man from the house said to Kramer.

They moved away, leaving Dawlish where he was. No one else seemed to be near, the pilot had gone into the house. They followed, and footsteps sounded on the wooden steps and the verandah, then a door banged, and there was silence. The sun burned down on to the back of Dawlish's head. He stared towards the river and the black shadow. If he could get to his feet and stay on them he could reach the shade, bring that distance down to fifty feet again. Getting up with his hands so tightly bound behind him wouldn't be easy, even without the cramp still in his legs and the pain in his head. He turned over on to his side, and, moving carefully, struggled to his knees; from his knees it would be simpler.

He reached them; it wasn't so easy after that as he'd hoped, but he got to his feet. Sweat ran off him. He could have run ten miles and felt no worse. He stood quite still, until the dizziness faded, and then stepped slowly towards the beckoning shade. All the time he wondered what they would do next. He could not see them without turning round and that would waste effort. Nothing had ever been so desirable as that shade; it beckoned as a woman full of promise. It was the only thing in the world. Sight and thought of coolness made the heat seem worse. Now it was only a few feet away.

He reached it.

It was like balm on an open wound.

The branches were high, the round trunks firm as the wall of a house. He went towards the nearest, reached it and leaned against it. Now he could see the width of the river, the rifts of sand on either side, the white tide-marks of the alkali dust on the cracked, baked bed. Now that he had the shade and the coolness, he wanted something else: water. His mouth felt as if he had been without drink for days. The water was so near. He moved away from the cottonwood trunk and went towards the river. He would have to go down on his knees, then flat on his stomach, with his mouth above the water; he could do that and he could get up again.

A man stepped out of the trees behind him.

"Going places?" the man asked mildly.

CHAPTER XVII
THE STAKES

HE WAS just another man, neither big nor small. He moved in front of Dawlish, who stopped walking. He wore an old ten-gallon hat and might have stepped out of a Wild West film, even to the week-old stubble and the half-smoked cigar jutting from the corner of his mouth, the hat-cord just above the point of his chin, the blue scarf tied loosely round his neck, the bright pink shirt and thick belt with guns on either side; even to the way his thumbs were linked over his belt.

Dawlish said, "That's right," and his voice was so cracked it wasn't recognizable. He turned slowly away from the man and began to walk towards the river, which was yards farther away in this direction. He knew that he wouldn't be allowed to reach it, but there was nothing in his mind except the need to try.

"Try it this way," the man said.

He was behind Dawlish again and the voice sounded very close. Then his hands dropped on to Dawlish's shoulders; one hand pulled, the other pushed. Dawlish twisted round, unable to help himself.

"And why don't you hurry?" The man pushed him in the small of the back, and he nearly fell; he regained his balance, and was pushed again. He stopped and reared up; the man pushed and didn't move him, came closer—and Dawlish back-heeled.

His heel caught the man on the knee, brought a gasp which told of pain. He knew that it wouldn't help, that it had been crazy to do it, but it gave him seconds of respite. He turned slowly and made for the river again, but that didn't last long. Two others came from the ranch, without hurrying; the one he had kicked went in front of him, shaking his leg to get rid of the pain; before he had grinned, now he looked as if this had become a personal feud. When the others reached him Dawlish was nearer the river than he had been before. One carried a two-pronged hay-fork. He went behind Dawlish and the fork pricked into his back; he just had to go where they wanted.

He knew despair. The shade fell behind him and the sun burned down. He staggered towards the ranch. His despair lifted; perhaps they were going to take him inside, anywhere out of the burning sun would be sanctuary. The pricking stopped when he was twenty feet away from the house.

Kramer stood at a window, his face blurred behind the mesh frame.

The handle of the fork smacked cruelly behind Dawlish's knees, and he crumpled up into the sand.

The men walked away, one to go back to the cottonwoods, two to the house, The front door opened and Kramer appeared. It was shady on the verandah, where two chairs and a table stood. Kramer brought out another chair. One man disappeared to return with a tray, bottles, glasses and a pitcher of water. They sat round the table and the water gurgled out of the pitcher. The men began to talk.

"When's he coming?" one asked Kramer.

"You can ask me."

"He coming himself?" the third man asked.

"Could be."

"Is it Clay?"

Kramer said, "Maybe it's Clay."

"Clay always was big-time."

"What started all this?" one of the men asked. They were just men to Dawlish, shapes he would see when he looked towards the house. All he could think about was the heat; and there was no escape from it. At a corner there was shade from the roof of the house. He started to crawl towards it. None of the men appeared to take any notice of him, they just kept talking.

"Who cares?" Kramer asked. "You're making a pile."

"I'm asking, when did the trouble start?"

"With Dawlish?"

"Someone saw Newton pushed over the Canyon. It was Dawlish's wife."

Dawlish stopped crawling, and twisted his head to look at the trio, but not one was looking at him. Kramer drained his glass. Dawlish's lips felt as if they were already swollen and his mouth was like sandpaper.

"That was her bad luck."

"You can call it luck. Forget it, we'll have to go over it all again when he comes," Kramer said. "You been to 'Frisco this trip?"

"Sure." They began to talk idly, lazily, about things that did not matter. Dawlish turned his head away and started to crawl again, fighting against the certainty that when he found shade they would drag him back; but even a few minutes out of the sun would be worth this effort. He covered the ground inches at a time, trying to fool them, although he knew that nothing he did would do that. He kept thinking about Felicity and what he now knew, although it didn't obsess him as it had done; only the thought of coolness did. But Kramer had turned a guess into a fact. Newton had been pushed over the Canyon's rim and Felicity had seen it happen.

Why did it have to be Felicity?

He was within three feet of the shade, and crawled more quickly. He reached it. The burning sun couldn't get at him. He turned over on his side and bent his knees, finding some comfort. It was hot but not scorching, and all he needed now was drink. He could just see the table, the pitcher and the glasses; they were there, but the men might have been a hundred miles away. To get drink he would have to cross that patch of ground which shimmered in the heat. He lay and stared, hypnotized. It surprised him, vaguely, that they hadn't stopped him this time.

He saw them get up and go into the house; the water and the bottles were there for the taking. He shook his head. If he reached the steps, crawled up them and reached the verandah, he wouldn't be able to drink, he would just spill the water. The river was his hope. It was farther away and there were a hundred feet or more of sun-scorched dusty ground to cross before he could get to the cottonwoods, and a hundred feet from the first tree to the river.

He had to try.

No one appeared to be watching him. He struggled to get to his knees again, succeeded, and got to his feet. He was near enough to the rail of the verandah to stagger to it and lean there for a rest. He looked at the table and then at the river. Men came from the back of the house, passed within a few feet but took no notice of him. They were carrying pieces of wood—fencing stakes, he thought—and one carried a big hammer, more like a sledge-hammer than anything else he knew. He watched them without wondering whether this had anything to do with him.

He started to walk towards the trees, a step at a time, because there was so little strength in his legs and he didn't want to fall again. When he wasn't staring at the silver ribbon of water as it flashed and beckoned from beyond the trees, he glanced at the men. They had stopped at a point between the house and the trees, and dropped the posts, separately. Then two held one post firmly and the third began to drive it in.

Dawlish still didn't connect what they were doing with himself. They were ignoring him, and nothing else mattered. He was near the trees.

He reached them.

The thudding of the hammer on the stake went on for a long

time, but stopped at last. He walked more quickly, hope giving him confidence—they might let him get one drink, just one drink; he didn't pause to ask why they should. He heard the rippling of the water, then more thudding; they were driving in another stake. Why?

Forget it. The river was only twenty feet away from him, and at the nearest point there was some shade from the tall cottonwoods. He must be very careful not to fall now; a fall would be disastrous. He looked right and left but saw no one watching, no one who could come and drag him away. He had passed no one.

He reached the water's edge, and began to tremble. Slowly he got down on one knee, then the other. The water shimmered and danced in front of him, crystal clear. He let himself go forward slowly until he lay flat, his face a few inches away from the water. He wriggled forward, and lowered his face and the water touched him, cool and desirable above all things. It filled his mouth and brought blessed relief. He swallowed some, and lowered his head again. He didn't pause to ask why they had let him do this, after they had brought him away once. Here was the water, the only thing he needed—he could lie and feel the coolness sinking into him.

He felt a tug at his legs.

He twisted his head, and saw two men bending down behind him, handling a rope. He felt the rope go over his ankles and drawn tight. He dipped his face into the water again and filled his mouth—and water spilled out as he was jerked away from it. He couldn't look behind him now, and see a man with a rope over his shoulder tied to his right leg; another with the rope tied to his left leg. They dragged him along as a horse would drag a cart. The sandy soil didn't hurt, and Dawlish held his face above it, but dust got into his lips, his mouth, his nose and eyes, he became parched again, felt far worse than before the drink.

They stopped at the edge of the trees. He hadn't seen Kramer come from the house, but it was Kramer who spoke.

"Who sent you out here, Dawlish?"

Dawlish closed his eyes and let his head fall to the ground so that there was no strain at his neck. He muttered:

"Where's my wife?"

"Who sent you, Dawlish?"

"Is she here?"

"Dawlish, do some listening. If you tell us who sent you, you can have rest, as much drink as you want—why, you can have a shower," Kramer said, and his voice rose. "Sure you can have a shower—water pouring all over you. Wouldn't that be just grand? Just imagine standing under a shower of cool water. Who sent you, Dawlish?"

"Is—my wife here?"

"Just answer my question, Dawlish. If you do, everything will be fine, maybe you'll see your wife again. Maybe. I guess it's probable. But if you don't tell us who sent you, then I want to tell you what will happen next. You'll be taken out and tied to those stakes, and your clothes will be cut off you, and the sun will fry you. So be a wise guy, and open up. Who sent you?"

"*No one sent me!*" He hadn't meant to say it, the words came out like a flood. "*No one*——"

"Okay," Kramer said. He wasn't talking to Dawlish.

After a moment's pause the ropes tugged against Dawlish's legs again. He was pulled more rapidly, out of the shade and into the glare of the burning heat. There were three men and they could do what they liked with him. They stopped dragging, two pushed him over to one side, and for the first time the handcuffs were taken away, but his arms were like withered flesh and he could not move them. They tied ropes round his wrists and his ankles, and pulled. He lay on his back with the sun beating on him, as they tied the ropes to the stakes, spread-eagled and as fast as he would be in death.

Kramer stood above him, with an open knife in his hand. He crouched down and slashed at Dawlish's shirt, then pulled and tore it away, cut the cellular singlet to shreds, tossed them aside, and then backed away.

"He won't last long," another man said. "He's halfway to talking already."

They moved off.

Dawlish closed his eyes but the sun burned through his lids. He felt it fierce on his chest and arms, his face and head; the right side of his head seemed on fire.

How could he make them release him?

He felt the fire in his head and agony in his body, and he knew he couldn't last for long; he would go mad, mad, mad. He turned his head, wildly, helplessly, heard himself groaning.

He'd do anything, say anything, to make them cut him free.

But he couldn't give them the answer they wanted. No one had sent him, he had come for Felicity.

Suddenly, the torment in his mind ceased and he lay still.

CHAPTER XVIII

BARGAIN

AFTER that onrush of panic and the fierce desire to submit Dawlish felt empty; as if fear had been drawn out of him. For a while he lay without conscious thought, accepting the burning because there was nothing else he could do. Then something akin to reason crept into his mind. They wanted him to talk and so they wouldn't leave him here long enough to drive him off his head. Hold on to that. This was bound to be short-lived. When they believed they had learned everything he could tell them, there was no end to what they might do; for they hated. But he need not fear yet, he was still in the hunt. He could fool them; he had to.

Two men came back, and Kramer was one of them. Even the shadow of the man's head and shoulders over Dawlish's face brought relief.

"Had enough, Dawlish?"

He didn't open his eyes.

"You can roast for a long time yet," Kramer said. "Who sent you?"

Dawlish kept his eyes closed and muttered; they wouldn't be able to understand what he said.

"What's that?"

He opened his eyes and glared, raised his voice and shouted words which made no sense. He stopped shouting, muttered a hoarse gibberish and began to turn his head this way and that. Kramer spoke almost uneasily.

"I don't like it."

"I told you he wouldn't last long."

"It's been no time."

"Look at the mess his head's in," the other man said. "He'll talk when he comes round."

"I don't trust him," Kramer growled. "I never have trusted

him." He was still uneasy, and he reached a decision quickly. "Bring him in."

"Okay."

Dawlish opened his eyes again and glared as a madman might, and began to shout and rave. He was still raving when men hurried out, cut him free, and carried him into the house. He raved in the house, when they put him on a bed in a big room and tied his wrists to the posts but left his legs free. He struggled wildly as soon as they had tied him and when they knew that there was no danger, so they weren't likely to use more violence. Kramer himself brought in water and sponged his face, let a trickle of water pass between his lips, then bathed his head, where it burned so. Then they went out. Dawlish let the ravings die away to a senseless mutter, then fell silent, watching the door.

Yes, they could still be fooled, but for how long?

"It must be those head wounds," Kramer said just outside. "If we've gone too far . . ." He paused, and then muttered angrily, "I still don't trust him."

The other man was confident. "He'll talk."

It was cool and there was no fierce glare, the bed was soft and he could relax; there was even the stimulus of this proof that Kramer didn't want to drive him out of his wits.

Who did they think had sent him?

What were they doing?

Both questions had thrust themselves into his mind before and been rejected, because the answers were unimportant until he knew what had happened to Felicity. Now they became too urgent to be easily thrust aside. What could they be doing, to go to such lengths as these? Until he had arrived at the Canyon, they had been working quietly; as far as he knew—as far as Morgan knew—no one had suspected crime, any kind of villainy. It had flared up partly because they were so desperately anxious to know who had sent him, but Felicity had really started it.

He lay quiet for a while. He heard a chair scrape, and a man stamped heavily in. Dawlish kept his eyes closed. When he heard the man going out, he opened his eyes and saw Kramer's back; probably Kramer was glad that he was dozing. Kramer wasn't sure whether Clay was the boss, but something in the past day or so had made him think it possible, and the other man seemed sure.

Dawlish dozed off.

He felt no pain from the sunburn, and doubted if he would; that summer, he had bathed and lazed on English and on French beaches, hardening his skin. Another hour, and he would have been agonizingly burned, but Kramer wouldn't give him another hour. Even his head ached less.

He was dozing when a new sound broke through into his consciousness: hoofbeats. He opened his eyes. They drew nearer, and soon horses stopped, men called out, there were footsteps on the floor of the big room, then voices from the verandah. He couldn't understand anything that was said. He wasn't left alone much longer. The footsteps came again and then Kramer appeared. Dawlish had expected to see Clay, but there was no sign of the gambler.

"So you're awake," Kramer said thinly.

"There's just one way you can get what you want."

"What's that?" How it mattered!

"Bring my wife," Dawlish said. "Bring her here."

Kramer didn't comment, just stood staring as if trying to make up his mind what to say. Then he turned on his heel and went out. Soon, others came in. They tied his legs to the foot of the bed and then unfastened his wrists. Cramp and pins and needles brought their own agony, but they passed. He was left to do what he liked. He hitched himself up, and pushed pillows into the small of his back, and sat in comfort. They didn't give him time to try to untie his legs; two men came back, one carrying a tray with two chicken sandwiches, iced water, coffee and wrapped sugar; why did wrapped sugar look absurd in the desert? One man pulled up a chair and sat down by the window; he had a gun in his holster.

The iced water stung Dawlish's mouth; he let it stay in his mouth until it warmed, and then he swallowed gently, and it was nectar. He drank a little more, then ate a sandwich, munching slowly. The bread was white and soft. He drank coffee and had another sandwich, and all the time felt more reassured than ever. Could this prove anything but their anxiety to keep him alive and alert?

"How about a cigarette?" he asked.

Kramer called from the next room. "What did he say?"

"He wants a cigarette."

"Okay." Kramer came in with a pack of Camels and a book of matches. He tossed them on to Dawlish's legs, stood watching as Dawlish lit one, and then said, "You know what will happen to you now if you don't talk."

"That's right," said Dawlish.

"Who sent you?"

"Where's my wife?" It was almost a refrain, but it could stop Kramer. He scowled and went out. It might mean that he knew Felicity was dead, couldn't produce her, and was beginning to wonder whether there was any other way of making Dawlish talk.

The taste of the tobacco was good. Dawlish smoked the two cigarettes, and then began to think about the lock of hair and the wedding ring, out in the blazing sun, in his shirt pocket. He saw a sun-dress, and then pictured Felicity in it. He saw her walking up the steps towards the Boeing that had taken her away from England. He imagined again her delight with everything she had seen here. He felt a false calm and knew that he must somehow retain it. He sipped more water and resisted the temptation to smoke another cigarette; there were eighteen left in the packet. He wished Clay would arrive—if Clay were coming. If he were here he would have shown up by now. Perhaps the horsemen had brought a message. There wouldn't be a road leading here, but couldn't cars be driven along the Canyon? Certainly the baked sides of the river were firm enough for a car, even for a truck. He was beginning to think 'truck' instead of 'lorry' after a ten-day spell. Cars, trucks, lorries or horses, what did it matter? There were plenty of ways of getting into this hide-away, but what about getting *out*?

If they were in a hurry they would use the helicopter again. They would be in trouble if the helicopter broke down. It wouldn't take much to make it; a handful of this sandy soil in the engine, for instance.

How many men were here?

One on the chair, looking as if he could fall asleep any minute. Kramer and the second man, the only other one who had done any talking, and two others—they were all he had seen. One, perhaps two, had arrived on horseback. When he added it all up, it just meant that thinking of throwing a handful of sand into the engine of the helicopter proved he was crazy.

Another man came in. The guard got up and went out, the newcomer took his place. He looked livelier. It was warm in here, much warmer than it had seemed when Dawlish had first arrived, but not hot enough to send the man to sleep. If he made a move to unfasten his ankles, the guard would come across at once, might tie his wrists and rob him of all chance of comfort.

There were no sounds in the rest of the house and none outside; just silence. It must be the middle of the afternoon. The guard had a wrist-watch.

"What time is it?" Dawlish asked.

"Time don't interest you."

"I'm just curious."

The man glanced at his watch. "Two-thirty."

"Thanks." Dawlish put out a hand for the cigarettes and matches. When he lit the cigarette and saw the flame it brought back the memory of the burning ranch—the first agonizing thought since the false calmness had descended on him. He let the match die out; the cigarette went out, too, but an idea was born. He lit another match and dropped it. The flame caught a paper serviette, he grabbed at it and pushed it to the floor.

"What the hell are you doing!" The guard jumped up and came across, treading the flames out. He was within arm's reach. Dawlish heaved himself across the bed and clawed at his throat, got both hands round it and squeezed.

It was crazy, but it broke the spell. Fierce exultation surged.

After the first choking gurgle the man made no sound, just struck wildly at Dawlish's wrists. His eyes showed the onslaught of fear; and no one had ever had a better reason for being afraid. Dawlish dug his thumbs and fingers into the leathery neck—then twisted.

The crack seemed loud.

Dawlish felt the guard go limp, but there might be another just outside; he didn't let him fall. He heard nothing, only silence came. He took one hand away from the twisted neck, supported the man with the other, knew that he was dead and thought no more of it than if he had killed a wasp. He pulled the man across the bed, over his own legs, then took a knife from a leather sheath. Wasn't this a bowie knife? He leaned forward, knife in hand, cut through the cords tying his ankles to the bed, then straightened up. He dared hardly breathe.

There wasn't a sound.

He lifted the man clumsily by the belt and lowered him to the floor, then drew his own legs up. Pain stabbed through them, but not so badly as it had done through his arms. He moved them slowly, and the bed creaked and the bedclothes rustled. He put the knife on the table, leaned over and took the gun out of the man's holster. Then he moved his legs off the bed and stood up.

His knees bent under him; he would have fallen but for the bed.

He stood upright for several seconds, gun in hand, then began to walk; it was painful but it wasn't impossible. He watched the open door all the time, but no one out there moved and he heard nothing.

He turned and looked down at the man on the floor; was sure that he was dead, bent down and felt his pulse; there was no movement. He walked to and fro, keeping as far away from the door as he could, and making little sound; but anyone who heard it would wonder what it was. The pain eased from his legs; he thought that he would be able to walk freely now; in emergency he might be able to run.

He went to the door.

Kramer sat near a window, chin lolling on his chest, obviously asleep. Dawlish tip-toed towards him; able to rely on his legs doing what he wanted. Kramer did not even know that he was being choked until the pressure was on. He started violently but hadn't time to struggle; Dawlish's vicious grip silenced and stilled but did not kill him.

Dawlish carried him into the bedroom, laid him face downwards on the bed, bound his wrists behind him, tied his ankles, stuffed the man's own handkerchief into his mouth, fastened it with his scarf, then took his gun and left him.

In the big room he paused to wipe the sweat off his face. Until then he had been so taut with the need for action that he hadn't consciously realized what had happened. He was free, had two guns, and two of the six men would cause no more trouble.

He fought back the sense of unreality; nothing that had happened since he had reached One Shoe ranch had seemed real; why should this?

He checked both guns; they were fully loaded.

The shutters were up at the windows, to keep off the heat of the sun, and there was no risk of being seen until he reached the door. He started for it, then glanced behind him; *think* man! There was a door on the right; the bedroom was on the left. He went swiftly towards the door on the right. It led to a kitchen and wash-house, and both were empty; the door leading into the open stood ajar. He reached it, crept out, saw the wall of the Canyon stretching up towards a sky of pale, steely blue. He walked, keeping close to the wall, until he reached a corner from which he could see the cottonwoods.

Some way off, the helicopter stood in the shade of the trees. Three men were in sight, one bending over the engine and two working at a table beneath a tree.

Where was the fourth man?

CHAPTER XIX

THE FOURTH MAN

DAWLISH could not see the fourth man.

He scanned the cottonwoods and the river, but saw no sign of him. There were more horses in the corral than when he had seen them before, standing and twitching their tails, coats dusty, heads down. Nearby were three outhouses, and the man might be in any of them. All were hidden from the helicopter by the house itself.

The burning heat hardly seemed to matter.

Dawlish went into each of the shacks, but no one was there.

He came out of the third and, in the shade it gave, studied the layout of the trees. He was twenty yards away from them at the nearest point, and for most of that distance he would be in full view of any of the three men near the helicopter if they happened to glance round; so twenty, say fifteen, yards were the dangerous ones. After that he would be able to get nearer to them while moving among the trees, and they weren't likely to see him.

He stepped into the sun.

The man bending over the engine straightened up and moved to the others; Dawlish backed out of sight. When he looked again, all three were bending over the table, as if intent on an engine part which had just been taken to it. Dawlish moved away from the shack and went quickly towards the trees, without running, looking at the trio all the time. He reached the cover of the trees, and the men were cut off from sight. He needn't worry about them now, only the fourth man mattered.

He had time to think.

The engine of the helicopter had been dismantled; or part of it had. He saw no car. If it came to it, he could ride one of the horses but he didn't know where to head, it would take a long time to get anywhere; he'd seen no other sign of habitation from the helicopter. So he ought to wait until that was ready for the air; he could pilot it, he'd handled small aircraft often enough. All he had to do was wait until they had finished. From here he could see both the back and the front doors of the house, and would know if anyone went towards it. If it weren't for the fourth man, all he needed was patience, and there was no end to his patience.

He heard a sound.

He spun round, facing the river; there was no one near, no one had seen him. But the fourth man was walking through the trees, buckets of water in each hand, and heading for the strip near the helicopter. Provided he stayed with them, nothing mattered but patience. There might be a man he hadn't reckoned on, but he thought that six was the limit. One dead, one bound and gagged, four over there. He moved over the soft earth towards them, until he was close enough to hear them talking; not that they talked much. He drew within fifty feet of them and leaned against a tree, a revolver in his right hand covering them. They weren't likely to see him, but they might. The man from the river had put his buckets down. One of them dipped a mug into the nearer one and drank; the others followed suit; then they doused their heads. After that all of them started to work on the engine; soon the parts were off the table and they were working at the helicopter itself.

Dawlish must have been waiting for an hour before one of them climbed in and tried the engine out. It turned over at the first attempt, the roar shattered the quiet and the trees seemed to shake.

It stopped. Dawlish saw the man climb out, and heard his drawled:

"It's okay."

"Let's go," another said.

They began to walk in a bunch towards the house, keeping to the edge of the trees so that they were in the shade. They didn't look towards Dawlish. He waited until they were almost level with him, and twenty feet away. Each had a gun in his belt; each could probably draw without conscious thought. He let them pass, then went swiftly, silently, behind them. They were ten feet ahead of him, three abreast and one a yard ahead, when he said:

"Stop walking. The first man who moves will get a bullet in the back."

. . . . .

They stopped as if someone had worked a switch. There was a moment of palpitating silence. Then the man just ahead of the other dropped his right hand to his gun and spun round. His gun was halfway out of his holster when Dawlish shot him through the chest. He let the gun drop, made a queer, tottering movement, but didn't fall at once. The echo of the shot seemed like thunder among the trees.

"Put your hands high," Dawlish ordered.

The man he'd shot tottered again, then pitched forward. One of the others tried to look round but made no attempt to get at his gun. Slowly, three pairs of hands went up; when they stopped there was no movement.

If anyone else were near, that shot would bring them.

Dawlish stood as still as the men in front of him.

. . . . .

No one else came.

That did not prove that no one else was near; one man, seeing what was happening, would keep out of sight; but there was probably no one.

"The man on the right," Dawlish said. "Take a step to the side."

The man obeyed.

"Take out your gun and throw it behind you." Dawlish was ready to fire again, but there was no need; the gun kicked up a little cloud of dust. None had any spirit left to fight with, and the man who had been shot lay very still. These might still have guns in shoulder holsters, but he doubted it; none had a coat. He went nearer. They knew what he was doing, and two of them glanced round but they didn't move apart from that. They didn't move until he struck them on the back of the head with the butt of the gun; he didn't need to strike any one of them twice.

Ten minutes later, each was tied to a different tree with ropes round their ankles, their waists and their shoulders.

The fourth man was dead.

Now Dawlish had to take a choice and it wasn't going to be easy. He could get Kramer away from here in the helicopter, fly until he saw a town, land just outside it, and go to the police; two hours should be enough for all that. Or he could wait to welcome Clay, or whoever these men expected. The one certain thing was that whoever came would come along the main gorge; the house was built so that there was no other approach, except along the river. From the verandah he could see anyone approaching a mile off or more. Before he decided what to do he would talk to Kramer, and the verandah was a good place for the interview.

Kramer was conscious.

Dawlish carried him into the big room, dumped him in a chair, then walked past him without a word, went into the kitchen where there was a pump over a big sink. He plugged the sink, half-filled it with water, pulled off the ragged remains of his undershirt and washed; even when he had finished grit still seemed to be in his eyes and mouth. He found ham, butter, bread and everything he needed for a quick meal in the big well-stocked larder; most of the stock was in cans. He cut ham and bread and took it into the big room, put a plate, knife and fork on the table, went back for beer which was stored in a tub of water, returned with it, pulled up a chair and started to eat. He heard the hum of insects as they came in through the open door but they weren't important; watching the trail was.

Kramer, still gagged, looked as if his eyes would pop out of his head.

Between mouthfuls, Dawlish said casually:

"Two of the others won't have to stand trial. They're with Bill Newton by now."

Kramer could show no reaction, except in his eyes.

"Three are tied to trees, Dawlish remarked, "and I don't bear any malice against them, they were paid for their job. So that leaves you, Kramer."

He went on eating, and Kramer followed every movement his knife and fork made, every movement of his mouth, every swallow. Dawlish drank deeply from a glass of beer, dabbed at his lips, and said:

"I've plenty of malice against you, Kramer. You and Clay.

After what happened at One Shoe, I could kill you the way you killed Eloise and no one would put me on trial for it. Do you think this place would burn easily? I do. There's plenty of gasoline to help make sure."

There was no colour in Kramer's cheeks but his forehead and upper lip dripped sweat, and he tried desperately to move. Dawlish finished eating, got up, took the bowie knife from his belt and stepped across to the prisoner. Kramer hadn't enough freedom of movement to cringe away. Dawlish played with the knife, then slashed at Kramer's face, keeping the blade an inch away. After that he cut through the scarf holding the gag into position, and pulled the gag out. He waited five minutes, then fetched water and poured some into the man's mouth. Kramer's lips looked so swollen that every movement must have been painful, and he made croaking sounds. Dawlish gave him another drink, then pulled up a chair and sat just in front of him.

"Is Clay coming here?"

"I don't know," Kramer said in a voice which wouldn't have reached a man standing on the other side of the room.

"Is Clay the boss?"

"I don't know that, either."

"Who are you expecting here?"

"The boss . . ." Kramer gulped. "I don't know who it is. I tell you I just don't know. There was a message this morning—one of the boys had it on the telephone, brought it here. The boss said he was coming. He was to be here around three."

It was now half past five.

Kramer was moving his lips grotesquely, as if the effort to talk had hurt him. He couldn't make himself look away from Dawlish's eyes.

"Something must have delayed him," Dawlish said dryly. "Where would he come from?"

"Huni City."

"How far away is that?"

"I guess it's thirty miles, between here and Las Vegas." If Dawlish judged the man rightly, there wasn't a thing he wouldn't talk about, if he knew anything about it. "It's just a one-eyed desert township, ain't on any main road."

"Police there?"

"Sure—sure there are police there." Kramer's voice seemed to hurt him every time he made a sound.

"Supposing you escaped from here, where would you go?" Dawlish asked.

It didn't put any hope into Kramer but it got an answer that seemed honest.

"I haven't any place to go now. I'd be on the run."

"So you'd be on the run," Dawlish mused. "That's fine. What did Newton see in the Canyon to make you kill him?"

"I didn't——"

"Okay, to make someone kill him."

"I wouldn't know. I think it was Clay who pushed him over, I'm not sure. I think he heard Clay and another guy talking, maybe the boss. I'm not sure, I tell you." He was almost crying. "I'm telling you all I can."

"Go on doing just that. Who do you think sent me?"

"I don't know that, either!" Was Dawlish right in believing that if the man did know, he would say? "The boss said he had to know."

"This boss you can't name?"

"He doesn't show himself!"

"He'll show himself," Dawlish said. "Why was he so anxious to know? What have you been doing? What's behind it all, Kramer?"

He didn't get an answer; perhaps he had asked too many questions at once. He stood up and went to the door, so as to get a better view of the trail. There was no cloud of dust, nothing to suggest that anyone was approaching. He saw two vultures perched on the man he had shot, pecking, and he saw others hovering. He sent a shot towards them and they flew off but they wouldn't go far. He hadn't thought of vultures. He felt sick as he turned back to Kramer, seeing the three men tied to the trees staring towards the body of the man who had taken the water to them.

"What have you been doing at the Canyon, Kramer?"

"We've been—prospecting," Kramer said. The words still came out as if they hurt. "Don't ask me what for. I don't know. We've taken samples of rock and sent them away for analysis. I can't tell you anything else, that's all I know. It had to be done so that Elliott's men didn't find out, but Newton found out."

"Leave it at that," Dawlish said. "Did my wife see Newton thrown over the Canyon?"

Kramer drew in his breath. "Yeh—yeh, that's it."

"Did you throw her over, too?"

As he asked that it seemed as if steel bands were fastening round him, and even breathing was difficult; but his voice didn't change. Kramer's expression did; he looked desperate, as if he knew that nothing had mattered so much as this—and with Dawlish nothing ever would.

"She wasn't thrown over! She was brought away. The boss thought she had come to snoop around, thought she put Newton up to watching."

"Why should he think that?" Dawlish asked. He went nearer to Kramer, his fists were clenched by his sides. "All right, leave that. Is she alive?"

"She was alive last night," Kramer gasped, "I saw her, she was at One Shoe ranch. *I* didn't kill her, I didn't take her away."

Dawlish stood close to horror.

Her dress had been there; she might have been at the ranch while he had been in Las Vegas, waiting for the dawn. If she had been alive then, she might be now.

And she might have been in the ranch-house while it had burned.

Dawlish moved away from Kramer stiffly, went to the door again—and in the distance he saw a cloud of dust along the Canyon trail, no bigger than his own hand.

CHAPTER XX
THE DUST

DAWLISH stood in the doorway. The dust was not dust but smoke, and beneath it there was the red hell of burning. His grip on the side of the door was so tight that it cut into his hand. He fought horror back.

There was not one cloud of dust, but three. Three cars or three horses? They were too far away for him to see. He didn't move. Kramer called out in a cracked voice, but Dawlish did not hear what he said. The clouds drew nearer, and soon he was able to see the tiny dots—horses, not cars. Beyond them he saw more dust, tiny clouds on a skyline turned now from steely blue to pale lavender. Over the land a softening haze spread, touching the distant walls of the Canyon with purple and mauve which seemed to take the heat away.

Dawlish felt the coolness but did not see the cause, only the fact that too many men were coming for him to fight alone.

He went into the big room, thrust his gun into his belt, lifted Kramer and carried him over his shoulder, into the sun and then the shade, towards the helicopter. The nearest horseman was still ten minutes' ride away. He dumped Kramer into the little cabin where he had been doubled up, and sat at the controls. He handled them and was more than ever sure that he could get the machine up in the air; a crash-landing wouldn't do all that harm.

But was Clay coming?

Clay would know the truth about Felicity, wouldn't he? If Dawlish flew off now he might lose his chance of discovering that truth.

Dawlish climbed down from the helicopter. The vultures still pecked at the flesh of the man he had killed, and the three men tied to the trees could only watch—the carrion birds or Dawlish or the clouds of dust which brought them hope. Gradually, sound came from the trail through the Canyon, the thump of hooves. The sun lay behind the ranch-house, shining into the eyes of the approaching riders. Dawlish judged that he would have time to see the first three and make sure that Clay was among them. He went no further than that, had no idea what he would do if he saw the gambler.

Eyes narrowed, he watched as the dots became men and horses, the men took on shape, the faces took on features. Eight men rode between the red sandstone walls, along the river where the water was purple and mauve except where the higher rocks, carved to strange shapes, reflected in the smooth surface. It was as if a master painter had used the Canyon and the desert for his canvas.

One of the first three riders was Sheriff Morgan.

• • • • •

Dawlish walked out of the shade of the trees and the helicopter, thumbs linked over his belt. He didn't recognize either of the two riders with Morgan, but was able to count five riding together some way behind. With the sun in his eyes, Morgan wouldn't be able to recognize him easily. Dawlish stood still. Morgan was no more than fifty yards away when he saw who it was. "It's Dawlish," came faintly to Dawlish's ears. The riders slowed down, and a yard away from Dawlish, Morgan stopped and swung himself off the saddle, supple as a man half his age.

His gaze fastened on to the side of Dawlish's head, and then travelled to the dead man, the trio tied to the cottonwoods and to Kramer in the cabin. He didn't smile, but there was warmth in his eyes; hope, too.

"Have you found her?"

Dawlish shook his head.

"You will," Morgan said slowly. "I don't believe any man could try as you're trying and fail. If you can talk, talk while we're attending to that head of yours. Anyone else at home?"

"There's a man with a broken neck," Dawlish said. He glanced at the other two riders, who nodded, then headed for the vultures; shots sent the gaunt foul birds away, to hover patiently in the cooling sky. The party of five was much closer now. "So this is what's called a Sheriff's posse."

"Don't get ideas, they're not my men. They're from Huni City." Morgan began to walk with Dawlish towards the ranch-house. "I suppose that's Kramer. Kramer thought that the helicopter was one sure way of escaping, he didn't realize that finding out where it didn't go helped almost as much as knowing where it did."

"Really?" Dawlish stopped near the four stakes, bent down and picked up a fragment of his shirt, slashed by Kramer's knife. He felt in the pocket and found the ring and silky hair. If Morgan had discovered the charred body of a second woman at One Shoe, he wouldn't have asked if Felicity had been found—would he?

"It wasn't seen flying over any town," Morgan went on, "so we drew a line from one town to another and said that maybe it was inside the area we marked off that way. A cattle-man near Huni told of a helicopter he'd seen disappear some-where near Huni Canyon—that's where we are—twice before. He didn't see it today, but it was worth trying, and we tried." They were on the verandah; Morgan led the way in. "Sit down, friend." Dawlish sat down, Morgan went into the kitchen and water splashed. Two men came in as he returned with a bowl of water and towels. Morgan washed the side of Dawlish's head, and gentleness couldn't prevent the pain. He prodded, still gently, sniffed, and went off again, coming back with a first-aid box. He bathed the lacerations with a soothing lotion, without talking. The others went in to see the man with a broken neck.

"Now I'll find out if I can still bandage a head," said Morgan. "You haven't exactly been talkative yet."

"What is there to say?" Dawlish asked wearily. "They brought me here and they were careless just long enough to give me a break."

"They tie you up to those posts out there?" Morgan's voice was very soft.

"When they thought I was going mad they cut me free. They still want to know who sent me—and no one did, Morgan."

Morgan nodded, as if he were convinced of that at last.

"Kramer talked. He says that they've been prospecting at the Grand Canyon, but he doesn't know what for. Bill Newton found out. Felicity saw Clay push Newton over. They think Felicity had come to spy. I'm past thinking why they should. What did you find at One Shoe?"

Morgan's lips began to twist in the smile that Dawlish had come to know as reassuring.

"A very frightened woman, I guess. Maybe in future she'll choose her friends more carefully. Eloise Day was lucky. The flames were licking along the floor towards the chair she was chained to. Ten minutes later, maybe five, she would have been burned up. She collapsed when we got her out, partly from the smoke, partly from shock. She's at the hospital in Las Vegas, when I came away she was still unconscious. We got Pop Rinker, of course, Pop never was as honest as he should have been. One Shoe's been used for a hide-out and for rustling. He named Kramer.

"Only Kramer?"

"Yes."

"Where's Clay?"

"We talked to Trig Clay," Morgan said almost casually. "He whipped his lady-friend, so what? He didn't take her away, he didn't know where she had gone. He had a fight with you at the Canyon but who started that? Not Trig Clay. He had been paid to follow you, and after the fight he walked out on Kramer, who paid him. He hired himself to Kramer because he had lost a big pile at the tables, decided to get out of Las Vegas for a time. He'd lost a pile, we checked that. He said he didn't know what Kramer wanted you for. He doesn't know a thing about your wife. He doesn't know about One Shoe. If we wanted to hold him, okay, hold him. Where's the crime in following a man and reporting where he goes and what he does? Sure he beat up his girl-friend. Okay, if he's the first man in the world to do that, hold him. He doesn't mind being held."

Morgan stopped.

"So he's still free?"

"Isn't that the way you want him?"

Dawlish began to smile, although it hurt the side of his head. He hadn't seen the lacerations and he wondered how bad they were; they could have been worse, or Morgan would have talked about a hospital.

"Thanks," he said. "What will happen if Clay leaves Las Vegas before we get back?"

"He won't leave. Rather than let him go, the police will hold him, even in Las Vegas with his friends," Morgan said confidently. "He'll be there waiting for a talk with you." Morgan took a cigar out of his shirt pocket, stripped off the wrapper and bit off the end. He stuck it between his teeth but didn't light it. "There's one other thing you won't be sorry to hear, Dawlish."

"What?"

"Your wife was at One Shoe until yesterday. She was moved, so far as I can time it with Rinker's help, soon after Eloise told you about One Shoe. A man in a Pontiac sedan took her away. We're tracing all the Pontiac sedans seen around. It could help. And if they kept her alive until yesterday, would they kill her today?"

• • • • •

Dawlish and Morgan flew out of the Canyon, leaving Kramer with the Huni City posse. Dawlish was at the controls.

Beneath them evening had darkened the colours, purple and mauve filled the Canyon, rocks which rose sheer out of the desert, and the desert itself. There was no harsh, dazzling brightness now but a softness over the land, soothing, magical. It gave Dawlish a kind of solace; he looked to the dark horizon and saw lights here and there, and to the West a cluster of them; Las Vegas. It was almost dark when they landed, and the bump on landing jolted Dawlish's head into screaming agony. As he climbed out, it killed every thought except of pain.

Morgan drove him to the hospital, and talked to a young doctor while Dawlish sat in an upright chair, his eyes glassy and his cheeks livid with the pain. He knew why he was given a shot, but couldn't find speech. Firm, cool hands undressed him.

He felt unconsciousness sweeping over him, and prayed it would come faster.

It was broad daylight when he came round, in a darkened room. His head felt brittle but didn't ache. His left arm was stiff and his shoulders and chest were sore, but nothing was bad enough to prevent him from sitting up and ringing the bell by the side of the bed. The nurse who came in might have been a Hollywood starlet. She gave him a drink, promised him breakfast, told him that it was eleven o'clock and that he would have to stay where he was at least for that day. He didn't argue. He argued with the lanky intern who came in soon afterwards and told him that he would be a fool if he didn't stay put.

"I've been a fool all my life, why should I stop now?"

"I was warned about you," the intern said dryly. "Stay there at least until Sheriff Morgan's been to see you."

"That depends on how long Morgan is." Dawlish could grin.

Morgan arrived at half past twelve, after Dawlish had breakfasted off boiled eggs and toast and butter, with weak coffee. Morgan had on a clean green shirt, he'd shaved, his cigar was half-smoked, his skin looked as if it would soon fall into brittle pieces, and his small grey eyes held a mildly humorous gleam.

"Clay's still here," he said.

Urgency took a grip on Dawlish.

"That Pontiac?"

"It hasn't got us anywhere yet."

"Are you tracing Clay's movements? Kramer's? Are you looking for——"

"Sure, the job's being done," Morgan said. "You forget we've had to deal with bad men before, friend."

Dawlish grunted, "Sorry."

"You don't have to be sorry. I understand. We haven't got far yet. Maybe Eloise Day can tell us something about Clay we haven't been able to find from anywhere else. She's in this same hospital, and she's part of the way to being herself again, if that's a good thing. She seemed mighty pleased to hear that you were okay. She hates Clay so much I think if we were to let her loose she would go and shoot him, so she's likely to be held here for a day or two. It would be friendly of you to go and say hallo."

"I will. Then I'm going to get out of here."

"If I can believe the doctor; you'll be able to handle any situation better tomorrow than you can today. Clay won't get away, not unless he tries to shoot himself out of town, and if he did that he would be on the run. He doesn't seem to me like a man who wants to run, he would prefer to sit back and let it all blow over. Clay will be waiting for you whenever you're ready."

"I'll stay here until after dark," Dawlish said mulishly. "It won't be so hot then."

Morgan shrugged.

Eloise, without make-up, with her flaming hair drawn back from her forehead and tied in a horse's tail at the back, and wearing hospital pyjamas, looked as if a day and a night had added ten years to her age. The shock from the fear of death still showed in her eyes. She talked a lot about Clay and what she would do to Clay, and Dawlish left her with an uneasy feeling that it wouldn't take much to turn her mind. As he walked along the cool corridors of the hospital towards his own room, he pictured her as he had seen her in Clay's shack; and standing and watching him through her lashes. Fooling who? Probably she would begin to mend if Clay were dead; until Clay died, there would be such hatred in her that she wouldn't see anything straight.

Then he wondered if she had talked too much; whether she was as bad as she made out.

What had Clay done to Felicity?

Morgan arrived just after seven o'clock. The film starlet nurse and the laconic intern were there to warn Dawlish to take things easily. His head wasn't back to normal and was hot beneath the bandages, but he felt as if he could face Clay or anyone.

"I've booked a room for you at the Gamblers," Morgan said. "It's on the same floor as Clay's. If you see men standing around they might be Clay's or they might be police. We're taking good care of you, friend. Remember I want to get Clay on a murder rap but it doesn't have to be for your murder."

"I'll remember," Dawlish said.

He was in his hotel room at half past seven; outside Clay's door ten minutes later.

CHAPTER XXI

BLUFF

Two men watched Dawlish as he stood outside the door of Clay's apartment, with the echo of his knocking still sounding. Neither of them spoke to him. He heard movements inside the room and wasn't surprised when a man who wasn't Clay opened the door. The man looked at him as if he would like to make him vanish into thin air.

"Is Clay in?"

"He won't be in to you."

"Listen," said Dawlish, "we've gone too far along this road for me to argue with a legman." He stepped forward and the man moved aside. This room was a sitting-room; two doors opened from it. Like the rest of the hotel, it gave an impression of opulence; thick carpets, ornate light-fittings, luxurious chairs and air-conditioning which made it pleasant to move about.

"Trig," the doorman called, "it's the limey."

He looked towards the open door on the right and Dawlish went across to it. Clay appeared when he was within a step of the other room. Clay still had his arm in the sling, and he moved awkwardly. His right eye was black and blue and there was a swelling on the side of his long jaw. His eyes were dull and he looked almost like a man who was walking in his sleep. For the first time, Dawlish doubted whether he was the big shot.

He had to be; if he wasn't Felicity was no nearer.

"So you've come," he said. "You're wasting your time."

"I've plenty of time to waste." Dawlish backed to a chair and sat on the arm. The doorman stared at his bandaged head and Clay looked at him as if he hardly saw him. This was an act with Clay. Wasn't it? "You know what I want."

"I told you all I knew about your wife."

"Sure?"

"I told you," Clay said. "I'm through with Kramer, through with all rackets. You can get out."

Dawlish slid off the arm of the chair and into its deep comfort. He took out a packet of Pall Malls and lit a cigarette, blew smoke slowly out of the corner of his mouth and watched it fade into a pale grey cloud. He sensed the impatience of the man at the door but did not think there was any risk of violence. There might be outside, but not here.

"If I leave without taking what I want," he said, "I shall go straight to the police."

"There isn't a thing they can fix on me."

"There wasn't," Dawlish said. He drew at the cigarette again —and he won a stab of interest.

Clay frowned. "There isn't." His voice sharpened.

"That was before I escaped from Kramer."

"You know what I think of Kramer?" asked Clay. "I think he's a small-time crook who reckons he's big. I made a mistake in working for him, and I don't make the same mistake twice. Why don't you go back to England, Dawlish? You'll be safer in England than you are here, I can't make the journey for a while." The threat was there, but was almost impersonal. Seeing him more closely, Dawlish thought that Clay looked tired, perhaps a sick man. The doubts came again and he thrust them back.

"After I left Kramer, I did some thinking," Dawlish said. "On how to fix you. I found a way."

"There isn't a way." Clay moved back, as if Dawlish's eyes were too close to his. "If you want to know what I told Morgan and the home-town police, go and ask them. I won't waste my breath. I didn't come and see you, you came to see me. There isn't a thing you know that's new."

"Did anyone ever tell you that the police want to hold you for murder?"

"Oh, sure. Only they can't find anyone I murdered."

"Kramer says you pushed Newton over the edge of the Canyon."

"Kramer would frame anyone to try and save his own neck."

"My wife saw you."

"I can't stop you guessing, I can't even make you guess right."

"Someone else saw you," Dawlish said flatly. "Someone I paid to keep quiet until I say talk."

No one else had, but it rattled Clay. A hint of expression crept into his eyes and he didn't speak. The silence might have meant anything. Dawlish waited for Clay to break it but Clay was a believer in keeping his mouth shut. Who else might have seen him? Who else could be named and be convincing? The question was hardly in Dawlish's mind before he knew the answer. He settled back more comfortably in his chair, crossed his legs, stubbed out the cigarette in an ash-tray which looked like a roulette wheel.

"Now you can start guessing," he taunted. "And I'll start talking. When my wife's back I'm going home. If I don't get her back, I'm going to wait here until you're hanged. I'm going to let that witness loose. It will be easy. That witness can hang you, Clay. But I'm not interested in why you killed Newton or what you're doing. I want my wife back."

He hoped Clay would ask, "Who sent you?" Clay didn't. Clay turned away, went to a chair on the other side of the room, and said flatly:

"There isn't any witness to something I didn't do."

"Try thinking more about it," advised Dawlish earnestly. "And don't forget I'm making an offer. My wife in return for a witness who won't talk." He stood up quickly, walked across to Clay, and put out his right hand. The doorman moved quickly, saying, "Hold it!" Dawlish ignored him. His fingers tightened on Clay's uninjured shoulder, and bit deeply enough to hurt; all the strength he had was in that grip. "Even if you killed me you wouldn't be rid of that second witness, Clay."

He turned, shouldered the doorman away and let himself out. He still looked savage as he walked past the two men watching from the outside, but it wasn't so easy when he was at the door of his own room, and they couldn't see his face. All this was like punching at a man who wasn't there. He couldn't even be sure that Clay was the big shot; Kramer hadn't been sure. If Clay were as bad as Morgan thought, as he knew, Clay might feel a net closing round him and take risks to break it that he wouldn't usually take, but would that lead to Felicity?

Dawlish opened his door.

Morgan looked up from a chair near the side of the bed. His feet rested on the bed, and his high-heeled boots were newly polished. His hands were linked across his narrow chest, and he wore his big hat.

"You still alive?" he asked mildly.

Dawlish said: "I'm going to stay alive. I didn't get anything out of Clay, it was like talking to a corpse, but I managed once to breathe life into him." He was glad to be able to talk; Morgan always seemed to be at hand when he was most wanted. "I told him someone he didn't know about saw him push Newton into the Canyon. He didn't like the idea."

"You're certainly a man for ideas," conceded Morgan. "If there was anyone, we'd have known. Do you hope to get Clay chasing shadows?"

"I want to break him down. If he thinks I can produce another witness, he'll probably try to put that witness away."

Morgan considered.

"I think I agree with you about that," he conceded, "but he wouldn't try to do it himself. You can be sure he would use someone else. He would be reluctant to do it here but if necessary I think he would try. Did you name anyone?"

"I just put the idea into his head."

"I guess you've gone too deep for me this time," Morgan said. "Who do you think he'll . . ." He stopped, and his eyes widened, Dawlish hadn't seen them so big before. He got up and went to the telephone, his boots creaking. "Give me Police Headquarters," he said, and waited, looking at Dawlish even when he spoke again. "Hallo. Matt Sligo, please. . . . Sure." He didn't speak but his eyes remained very round and bright. "Hi, Matt, this is Morgan. You're having that hospital covered, aren't you? Nothing could happen to Eloise Day, could it? . . . Well, maybe you could make doubly sure, Matt." He rang off, stood leaning against the wall and grinning. "I don't know whether to be glad you're not an American citizen or to wish you were," he went on musingly. "Eloise was at the Canyon with Clay, so she's the most likely witness, but you've made one miscalculation. If she'd seen anything, she would have told us by now. Clay knows that. The fact that she hasn't is obvious to him, because we've done nothing to hold him. He knows we'd hold him if we had a witness."

"I told him I'd paid the witness to keep quiet—that I'd exchange the name for my wife," Dawlish said. Morgan took the cigar from one side of his mouth and put it in the other. "I'm glad you're taking care of Eloise, but why not do something else to make Clay think that she's the witness?"

"Don't you like Eloise?"

"I'm relying on you to look after her."

"What would you do if you had the doing of it?"

"Take her away from the hospital and hide her. When Clay's men go to try to get her, they'll find no one there. He has plenty of friends in Las Vegas, so it would be reasonable if some of them heard police officers saying that I'd taken her away. Wouldn't he think that likely?"

"Maybe," Morgan agreed thoughtfully. "He might ask where you would take her."

"To any one of a hundred motor-courts." Dawlish pushed his hand through his yellow hair above the bandage. "I'm thinking aloud, give me time." They watched each other. "If I leave Las Vegas with Eloise he'll be sure who that witness is, won't he? If I were to take her to the airfield under a police escort and get her away in a special 'plane he wouldn't be able to follow. If I came back here and he didn't know where Eloise was, he would probably come and try to make a deal. Am I crazy?"

"Don't tell me you've any doubt about that," said Morgan heavily. "Maybe it's worth trying. We've more thinking to do, where to send her——"

Dawlish broke in with a grin that was almost gay.

"As we're going to fool Clay, let's fool him properly. I'm to collect a woman from the hospital, she'll have her face covered when she comes out and when she gets to the airport. Anyone will do. Then Eloise will be in the one really safe place—the hospital which Clay thinks she's left."

He hadn't heard Morgan laugh before.

• • • • •

Dawlish and Morgan stood and watched the lights of the aircraft as it roared towards the stars. There were a dozen people about and they weren't all ground staff or airport officials. The car Dawlish and Morgan had driven from the hospital in was waiting for them. They had been followed from the hospital but they weren't followed back into Las Vegas. Morgan dropped Dawlish near the Big Stakes saloon, and drove off. Dawlish, a head taller than most of the people, moved among the throng beneath the flaming lights with their ever-changing colours, looked into the crowded saloons, the restaurants, the drug stores and the soda fountains. Everyone seemed hot and everyone seemed in a hurry to get finished eating or drinking and get back to the saloons. The city seemed more crowded and more unreal than the previous night.

Dawlish entered the Big Stakes, knew that he was closely watched, but didn't find Clay there. He went out, and the night was only slightly cooler than the saloon. He'd built the idea up in his mind until it had seemed a certain winner, but now he wasn't sure. He felt as if he would never be sure of anything again until he had found Felicity; or until he knew that he would never find her. After the exhilaration of the past hour, the reaction dropped him as low as he had ever been; his jaw hurt because his teeth were clamped so tightly together. Clay was a gambler above everything else, and a gambler's chief weapon was bluff. Why think that he could out-bluff a man who had spent his life learning the way to do it properly?

Dawlish went into a drug store, sat up at the soda-fountain and ordered coffee. As he smoked and drank he knew that he was watched from the door; there had hardly been a moment here when he had been free from watching eyes. Clay's men—who would never admit that they were Clay's men—as well as the police were there. If a thing were certain, it was that Morgan and the Las Vegas police did not mean to take any chances with him. Knowing that, Clay wouldn't take any risks, either.

If Clay had been bluffed he daren't take any risks. He would need to come to terms. He had to know who had sent Dawlish and he had to know whether Eloise had seen him murder Newton, and where she was. He would be sure that Dawlish was in a mood to sacrifice anyone and everything for his wife. *If* Clay had been bluffed, that was.

Dawlish went back to the Gamblers, followed all the time, stepped into welcome coolness, was taken up to the third floor and went to his own room. He wouldn't go to Clay again, it would serve no purpose. Clay would have to make the first move. If he were going to make it, he would probably make it tonight.

Two men were in sight of his door, and he didn't know which of them had a Sheriff's badge beneath his waistcoat. He went in. The big room was empty. He stripped and took a shower, with his ear cocked for the telephone, and it didn't ring. He dabbed himself dry, pulled on his pyjama trousers and lay on the bed, looking at the ceiling.

The telephone-bell rang.

He hesitated, and then lifted the receiver.

"Dawlish speaking."

"Get rid of that cop outside your door," Clay said. "I want to see you but I don't want Morgan or anyone else to know.

Fix it, Dawlish, if you want company when you go back to England."

"You come to me," Dawlish said. "Never mind the cop."

CHAPTER XXII

OFFER

DAWLISH opened the door and Clay came in slowly. Morgan's man and Clay's watched until the door closed. Dawlish pushed up a chair and Clay seemed glad to sit down. Nothing about him had altered, but the way he carried himself told of strapped ribs which still pained him.

"I could use a drink," he said.

"I've Scotch-and-soda."

"I'll drink it."

Dawlish poured drinks, and Clay watched as if hoping that he would see the big hands shaking. He didn't. Dawlish put Clay's drink on a table near him and went back to the bed, sitting down on it, keeping one hand in his pocket. His calmness was a brittle veneer which might break at any moment, and he was afraid of what he would do if it broke. Clay wouldn't have come here unless he could talk terms, and that meant he knew plenty about Felicity.

"Who is your witness?" Clay asked flatly. "Eloise?"

"I can't stop you from guessing."

Clay said: "Listen, Dawlish, you've got a lot of things wrong. You string along with the police too much. I don't know how much you've told them, but you can take it from me, if you've told them anything that would help them to hold me, you can kiss your wife good-bye."

"Morgan does the sticking, I can't shake him off," Dawlish said. "If you don't know by now that I want just one thing, it's time you gave up working. I told you before, Newton didn't mean a thing to me, what you were doing at the Canyon doesn't mean a thing, who dies and who lives doesn't mean a thing. I've told Morgan just enough to keep him happy. He wants you but can't get you. He could, with the witness."

"With Eloise?"

Dawlish didn't answer.

Clay said! "You want me to talk. You'll have to talk first."

"I don't see it that way."

"Your wife's alive," Clay said, very evenly. "She doesn't like the company and she doesn't like being a prisoner, but hasn't been hurt or treated rough—yet. I'll make an offer. Eloise for her."

Dawlish didn't trust himself to speak, sat there with his glass in his hands and his eyes telling Clay of his hatred; and beneath that, a seething hope.

"And for one other thing," Clay added. "Who sent you, Dawlish?"

"No one sent me."

"That's a lie."

"She came to visit friends, they lent her a car, she drove by herself because she wanted to see as much as she could of the States. She found a guide with enthusiasm for wild flowers at the Canyon, and discovered that he had been in England, married a girl from our home town. That's all."

"I don't believe it."

"All right," said Dawlish. "How does that get you out of the spot you're in?"

Clay said: "I don't believe you came here just to look for your wife. You're a private eye. You sent her first, you were coming anyway. You were working with the guide Newton. He was spying for the guy who put the black on me. Who is that guy, Dawlish?"

This was the first crack—cause for excitement, almost exultation. Clay was being blackmailed and thought Newton a legman for the blackmailer; and he might be right. He thought Felicity had come to see Newton on business; this blackmailing business. So a man Clay couldn't name had something on him, and he had to find out who. That was why he had taken such risks, why he would take more. Someone could frighten Trig Clay by striking at him viciously, out of the dark.

Why did he think Felicity knew? Or he, Dawlish?

This wasn't the moment to try to widen that crack, to tell Clay how much he'd given away. Let him think Dawlish knew more; let him grope as a blind man.

"Clay, I've had a lot of trouble with Morgan. He knows that I'll throw dust in his eyes, in anyone's eyes, to get my wife back. I didn't tell him why I sent Eloise away, just said that she was afraid of you and so I staged her getaway—saying she didn't feel safe in Las Vegas. Morgan can guess what he likes, but he doesn't know much yet. Try and get that into your head. And get this, too—I can tell Morgan everything any time I like. I have only to lift the telephone."

"So it was Eloise," Clay said softly. "The bitch. The double-crossing whore, she——" He broke off. There was such hate in his eyes that it was like a fire, throwing out heat.

"I've only to lift the telephone," Dawlish repeated.

Clay clamped his lips together, and his eyes dulled. There was nothing he hadn't admitted now, even if it couldn't yet be used in evidence. He could be blackmailed and so tormented that to catch the blackmailer he could take desperate risks. And he had provided more grounds for blackmail.

He was making the obvious guess now. The one person who might have seen him throw Newton over, who could have crept out of the hut and followed him to see why he had left his hut so early in the morning, was Eloise.

"And you paid her to keep quiet," he questioned harshly.

"I paid the witness."

"She won't keep quiet," Clay said. "She might until you've gone away, no longer. Not Eloise. She might help you find your wife, she could be that soft—she tried it once." He was talking to himself more than to Dawlish, and now his eyes burned again. He raised his voice sharply. "Okay, Dawlish, your wife in exchange for Eloise. And for information: who sent you? Who paid Newton to spy on what is happening at the Canyon? To spy on me."

Dawlish said: "The next move is seeing that I get my wife back, unhurt. Where is she? What was this talk about the redwoods and Highway 101?"

Clay said: "I wanted you to go there, to keep you away from the place that mattered. One Shoe." He brooded. "You'll get word in the morning where to go. You'll have Eloise with you when you arrive. The place is most of a day's journey from here. If Eloise isn't with you, I'll slit your wife's throat." He stood up, went to the door, and then came back halfway across the room. His face was a sultry fire. "Don't make any mistake, Dawlish. Shake off Morgan and anyone he sends after you, just be there with Eloise."

He went out and the door slammed.

• • • • •

It would be easy enough to see Morgan and talk to him; Clay couldn't be certain what they talked about. It would be easy to get Morgan's help again although it might not be so easy to make sure that Morgan took the Las Vegas men off.

Dawlish had believed in the beginning that this was his fight and would have to be fought alone; he'd been wrong most of the time; for the last act he might be right.

He had to get some things clear.

Taken at its surface value, Clay had offered to exchange Felicity for Eloise; one woman who had seen him murder Newton for another whom he believed had seen him. Scratch the surface and what showed? Clay wouldn't even think of doing it, was trying another bluff. While he had Felicity he thought he had a chance of luring Dawlish on to a last mistake. He might even persuade himself that for Felicity, Dawlish would take any risk, put himself in any den of lions, risk all three lives.

That was so obvious that it was hardly worth pondering; yet Dawlish made himself ponder. Out of the effort came a hope; that if Clay were dependent on the bluff succeeding, he was at his last ditch. Would even a desperate man think he had a chance? Clay was a gambler, so odds wouldn't worry him; chances were his life. Even allowing for that, could Clay seriously hope to get all three of them together? Or was he simply hoping to find a way of getting Eloise, and finding out who had blackmailed him before Bill Newton's death?

Dawlish sat brooding. Morgan would telephone soon and he hadn't decided how much he would tell the Sheriff. He didn't think Morgan would be surprised if he stalled, but he was sure Morgan would try to keep him watched all the time.

The telephone-bell rang.

"Dawlish."

"How did it go?" Morgan asked.

"He came to tell me that I was crazy, that he didn't know a thing," Dawlish stalled. "I'm no further ahead than I was when I started." It wasn't difficult to put bitterness into his voice, but that didn't mean that he sounded convincing. "I don't see what to do next, Sheriff, I'm all washed up."

"That so?" Morgan spoke musingly even on the telephone. "Friend, let me tell you something."

"Well?"

"If you try to handle this by yourself you'll be booking a

ticket to hell. And I'm not forgetting what happened at Huni Canyon. That can happen once, I'm almost convinced that it *did* happen once, but not twice. No, sir. You sleep on it, and change your mind in the morning."

"The trouble with this country is that everyone is too damned clever," Dawlish roared. "To hell with you all!"

He banged down the receiver. He didn't know whether the hotel operator had been listening in or whether a report would go to Clay, but he thought both were likely. He hoped that Clay's man outside had heard him. He took out the wedding-ring and ran the hair through his fingers, twice, very slowly. Then he felt in his coat pocket for the automatic, and the one fitted on the shoulder-holster. The roar at Morgan had broken a tension inside him.

After a while he knew exactly what to do. Make Clay believe he was going to gamble. Fool Clay, that was still the answer. It was a game of poker; neither could see the other's cards.

He moved towards the window, switching off the bedside light and leaving the room in darkness. He opened the window and looked out on to darkness; it faced a side street. A glow of light came from one direction but didn't matter. He peered down the wall, seeing the ledges at the windows; it was easy to climb. He clambered out of the window and went down without difficulty. On the ground he hesitated and then turned away from the lights at the main street, a hundred yards away.

He walked over two narrow streets, then saw more lights, stretching right and left; there were motor-courts and gasoline stations. He had four thousand dollars in his pocket and five hundred was enough to get him a self-drive Studebaker which had seen better days but had a turn of speed and venetian sun-blinds at the side windows. He drove towards the hospital and parked close to the main doors. There was no certainty that he wouldn't be seen by someone who would report to Clay, but there was no way of covering every angle. He walked in, nodded to a night clerk at the desk and went along the main corridor; the man didn't trouble to follow him. Eloise wasn't far away. He reached her room and hesitated outside it; no one appeared. He turned the handle and went inside; there was silence.

He closed the door without locking it, and went to the window; it was open, but the mesh frame was a fixture. Beneath the window was a big suit-case; they'd sent for her clothes, he didn't know from where. There was some light from a lamp outside, and gradually he got used to the gloom. Eloise slept on one side, facing the window. He sat lightly on the side of the bed. She was wearing nylon or silk; her own. Her right arm, bare from the shoulder, lay over the sheet which was pulled up almost to her chin. He put a hand on her arm and pressed gently, and she stirred. He moved his hand and held it over her lips, and she started violently. He felt her mouth open and her teeth brush against his palm.

"Keep quiet," he whispered. "Keep quiet."

She didn't try to free herself, but became very still. He took his hand away slowly, knowing that she had recognized him.

"Remember Trig Clay?" he asked, and her diatribe earlier in the day was vivid in his mind. She didn't answer, and he went on: "You want to see him dead, don't you? Hanged."

"I'd die to fix it," she said, and it was easy to believe her.

"There's a way, and it would give you a chance to stay alive."

"Wait just a minute." Eloise raised herself on her pillows, and, sitting up, her right hand searched for his and caught it. "A minute," she repeated, looking at him all the time. Then, "Okay, I'm wide awake now."

"He's offered me a deal," Dawlish told her. "My wife in exchange for you."

"For—*me*?"

"The day he pushed a Canyon ranger over the rim, you'd followed him and saw it happen."

Her hand stiffened in his, and then she snatched it away. She seemed to rear up, and he could hear her harsh breathing.

"You told him *that*?"

"Yes."

"So you've put me on the spot," Eloise said and her muted voice was vicious. "What have I done to you, what——"

"Take it easy. You and I are to be at a place where he'll tell us to go. Tomorrow. My wife will be there."

"You'd believe Clay?" She caught her breath. "I didn't think you could be fooled like that, I thought you were good. Forget it."

"You want to see Clay broken, don't you? My wife's the one witness who can break him. By getting her free you'll have Clay smashed into little pieces. I can't get her without you. The police can't pin this on to Clay without her." He paused, then gripped her shoulders, his fingers sinking into the warm, soft flesh. "I can't offer you another thing. I've no money here, not what you'd call money. I've nothing else at all. But this will give me a chance and you a chance of getting what we want. And unless someone gets Clay, he'll get you. You know that, don't you? He'll get you because he hates you as much as you hate him."

"You're mad," she breathed. "Raving."

"All right," said Dawlish. "You think he'll hold us all. I know he'll try. I know another thing. He's in a lot of trouble. He's been blackmailed. Did you know that?"

"Clay? Blackmailed?" She sounded as if she couldn't believe it.

"Blackmailed. He doesn't know who by. He thinks Newton was a spy for the blackmailer. He thinks my wife can name the blackmailer; and that I can, too. He has to find out. So my wife and I are safe until he knows—or until he realizes we can't tell him a thing. That gives us all a chance."

Eloise didn't speak.

"And here's another thing," Dawlish said. "If I can't make sure that the police get Clay, I'll kill him with my own hands. I can and you know I can. Here's your chance, Eloise, you haven't any other."

It was his chance, not hers; he felt sure that she would refuse, couldn't think of a good reason why she should agree. He got up, slowly, trying to find words that would persuade her but none that occurred to him seemed likely to have any effect. In the dim light he stared down at her, seeing it shine on her eyes, on her hair. Her beauty seemed to glow.

"You'll kill him," she said huskily.

He held up his hands.

"With these."

"I'll come," said Eloise.

"Get up and get dressed," Dawlish said. "We're getting out of here."

He wouldn't let her out of his sight until it was over. She knew that he didn't have the answer that Clay wanted, which meant that she knew too much.

He would start out, and Clay would think he was going all the way. But he didn't know how far he was going. Only one thing mattered: seeing Felicity again. He could go on from there.

CHAPTER XXIII

RENDEZVOUS

DAWLISH woke slowly, his mind hazy. He lay on his side, looking at an unfamiliar wall. Outside, the sun shone through the thin curtains at the window of a room he didn't remember seeing before. He hadn't seen it by day. He remembered what had brought him here, and stiffened, then turned slowly on to his back and looked at the next bed. That was a big one, his a single; a three-bedded room in a third-rate motor-court on the outskirts of Las Vegas.

Eloise lay on her side, looking at him, a thin sheet covering the rounded beauty of her body. Her knees were bent. The sheet was drawn just above the rich fullness of her breasts, but her arm was outside, as it had been when he had woken her at the hospital; her arm and shoulders were bare. She didn't smile as he looked at her. He let memory flood back into his mind, but he didn't look away.

Slowly she raised herself on her elbow, and the sheet slipped back.

"Hi, Pat," she said.

"Hi."

"This is the day when you're going to kill Clay. Remember?"

"I'll fix him or kill him."

"You think you will," she said. "Maybe you've a chance but it isn't the best chance in the world. It could be your last day alive. And mine."

"It won't work out like that."

"It could," Eloise said. "So we haven't much time. We could use what time we have." She wasn't smiling, but her eyes were calling him. That shouldn't surprise him; he had known that she was wanton, she hadn't hidden it, and she hid nothing now; neither what she could offer or what she desired and wanted him to desire.

He said: "I'm going to have a shower. You can get dressed while I'm gone." He pushed the sheet off him and got out of bed, picked up his undershirt and pants, turned away from her and went to the door of the shower. He stripped, turned on the cold tap, and water hissed and splashed. He was there ten minutes altogether, and when he went back into the bedroom she was wearing a pale green dress, sitting at the dressing-table and combing her hair. She looked at him sideways, smiling as if suddenly touched by innocence; she was good to look at.

"Hi," Dawlish said lightly. "Hungry?"

"So we're going to eat before we die."

"Who turned you into a pessimist?"

Her eyes glowed. "You did," she threw back. "Pat, I don't think there's another like you."

"You've mixed with the wrong people."

"I expect I always shall."

"Come back with Felicity and me and have a holiday in Europe," Dawlish said, still lightly. "When you come back you'll see America as I see it. The side that doesn't know anything about Trig Clays and Kramers. Or ask Sheriff Morgan to introduce you to some nice guys." He grinned.

"Everyone in the world can say 'nice guys' except you," Eloise said, and finished doing her hair. "It sounds phoney from you. Where are we going to eat?"

"There's a restaurant next door. I can't see Clay's men coming as far as this out of town. They think you're a thousand miles away and I'm still in my hotel." He slid into his trousers and shirt, sat on the bed and put on his shoes. "So you'll take the chance?"

"Didn't I say I would?"

"Let's go," Dawlish said.

After breakfast, he sent her back to the room, and went to a telephone booth in a corner of the restaurant. He called the Gamblers Hotel and asked for Clay. It was some time before Clay answered, and then his voice was heavy as with sleep; it wasn't yet eight o'clock.

"Who's that?"

"Dawlish."

"Daw——" Clay broke off; it was the first time he had really shown surprise.

"If I'm to shake Morgan off, I have to shake your men off, Dawlish said. "I left by a window soon after talking to you. Where am I to go to?"

"Where are you?"

"Just give me the rendezvous."

"How will you travel?"

"Just give me that address, Clay."

How much would Clay stake?

"Okay. Don't forget it. It's a farm just across the border, in California. A peach farm. There's a map waiting here for you, showing exactly where."

"I don't want a map."

"It's Pasadena Farm. You'll go through Santa Rosa and at the last street lights you'll turn left, drive for ten miles and come to Marita. Beyond Marita, you take the second to the right. Along there you'll see the signpost to the farm."

Dawlish said, "I've got that."

"Why don't you repeat it?"

"I don't have to."

"Dawlish, listen to me. If anyone else comes——"

"Just the two of us. Morgan was mad with me last night but he'll get over that."

"Where are you?"

Dawlish rang off. It would do Clay a lot of good to wonder whether he had staked too much. Clay was risking everything; but Clay had to risk everything, because he had everything to lose. He had his own hand hidden, too. He'd at least protect himself against Morgan; against simple trickery. Would he? The simple tricks were often the winners. The one thing it was obvious a man wouldn't do was exactly the thing to do. Such as walk into the lion's den; or the peach farm. Dawlish went to the car, took it to a gasoline station and filled up and got a map. By the time he was back at the motor-court he knew that it would be middle-afternoon before he could reach Pasadena Farm.

Eloise opened the door a crack, recognized him and opened it wider.

"Did you talk to him?" Whenever they were discussing Clay her face hardened.

"Yes. Did you know he had interests in a peach farm?"

"It wouldn't surprise me what he has interests in," Eloise said. "When do we start?"

"Now," said Dawlish. "You'll sit in front with me, we'll have the venetian blinds down, and we'll keep our fingers crossed until we're out of Las Vegas."

"How much about this do the police know?"

"Nothing."

She said half-admiringly, "You take big chances when you take them."

"It's a habit in these parts. I must have caught it."

"You want one thing, I want another," Eloise said thinly. "There are times when I wonder whether it's worth it." She looked at him oddly. He remembered the way she had looked at him through her lashes, and the fact that he had wondered who she was trying to fool—Clay or him? He had the same uneasy feeling that she was trying to fool someone. Could she think that she could win Clay round again? After what had happened? No, that didn't make sense, and there was no doubt that she hated. It was reasonable enough that she should believe that if they didn't get Clay, sooner or later he would get her. Why not forget those shadowy doubts?

Two couples and a family at the motor-court were getting ready to leave when Dawlish opened the door of the car for Eloise. A girl of about twelve, in pigtails, and a boy of six or seven, his head almost shaved except for a ridge which ran from his forehead to the nape of his neck, watched with the frank curiosity of children. A coloured girl collecting bed-linen glanced at them and smiled. A man in blue jeans and already looking hot stood at the exit as they drove out, and nodded to them casually. No one else seemed to take any notice.

Dawlish avoided the centre of the city, making a two-mile detour in order to get on to the road West.

It was already too hot. Warm air came in at the windows through the slits in the blinds. They had no air-cooler. The sun was behind them, and ten miles out of Las Vegas they pulled up the blinds; it made no difference except that the fuller stream of air coming in gave an illusory coolness. Dawlish put his foot down and kept it there. Rocks and flat-topped hills on either side were robbed of colour by the intense light of the sun. As they went out into the desert it was pale and harsh. Ranges of hills in the distance stood out against the metallic blue of the sky, aloof, uninviting.

No one followed them; no one tried to keep pace. The needle quivered between eighty and ninety. Except to glance at Dawlish, Eloise kept her gaze on the straight, flat road ahead. She looked cool, and the self-possession which had come that morning remained. She was hardly the same woman who had talked with shrill hatred of Clay the day before. He wasn't the man who had listened. Now he believed that Felicity was alive; that he might see her today. His mind refused to work beyond that. He tried to force it. Surely the last thing Clay would expect would be for him to take Eloise to the peach farm.

Supposing he did just that. Clay would have them, all three; but Clay would see a trap that wasn't there, and would be wary, hesitant. They would play out the final bluff; and Dawlish's hand was strengthened because Clay didn't know who was blackmailing him.

The sun rose higher and the heat grew worse, the car was oven-hot, and the wind off the desert carried with it a thin film of penetrating dust which settled on them and on to the dashboard, got into their eyes, mouths, noses. The back of Dawlish's seat was sticky with his sweat. He kept wiping his neck and forehead with a handkerchief which soon became a damp ball.

"Later it will get hot," Eloise said.

"Still a pessimist?"

"We're heading for Death Valley, and there isn't a hotter hellspot in the States. The only way to drive through it is at night."

"We can't wait."

"You really think you'll beat him, don't you?"

"I didn't come here to lose."

"I don't think you'll lose," Eloise said slowly, and then paused and corrected herself. "That isn't right, I guess. I don't *feel* that you'll lose, if I start thinking about it I know you haven't a chance."

"So you're backing your heart instead of your head."

"Just like you," she said.

He glanced at her, and was caught by her beauty and by the flame of her hair with the sun shining on it. Ahead, the road was an empty ribbon.

"I'd like to know what makes you blow hot, then cold. All weak and feminine one moment and an Amazon the next."

"You," she said promptly, seriously. "When I'm on my own and think of Clay, I'm terrified. Then you remind me that Clay can be thrown around like a garbage can, and I'm the world's heroine."

After a while, Dawlish said:

"What else?"

"You know everything, boss!"

But when he glanced at her again her eyes were clouded.

"Not yet, Eloise," he said quietly.

"I've always done that."

"What?"

"Blown hot, blown cold."

The heat lay upon and about them, and the wind they made seemed sluggish because of it. The glare of the sun was so fierce that it drew all colour out of the desert and the ranges of hills, small clouds of dust whirled about, close to the road and farther away, a hundred tiny whirlwinds. There was little traffic, just an occasional car and truck which passed them from the West; nothing overtook them. The road invited speed, and Dawlish had never been in a greater hurry.

They passed through the tiny desert township of Death Valley at noon, and directly they were on the other side Dawlish put his foot down and the needle shot past eighty again and stayed there. He was sitting in a bath of his own sweat. Eloise's face was shiny, she kept easing her position. At the next drive-in he decided that he would stop for a meal. Now and again they passed cars drawn up off the road. Each time he looked in the driving-mirror, half expecting a car to start after him, not fully convinced that he had escaped without being followed by either Clay or Morgan, or their men.

Nothing suggested that they were being followed.

. . . . .

They stopped for fruit inspection at the Californian border; it took three minutes. There was no difference in the country but they had already left the true desert behind. It seemed cooler, although Dawlish had almost forgotten there were degrees of heat.

At half past three Santa Rosa appeared on the signposts for the first time; thirty-one miles away. At four o'clock they drove into the city, just a string of garages, motor-courts and stores on either side of a wide road, with several side-streets, each of the cross-roads controlled by traffic lights. Dawlish couldn't mistake the last, and turned to the left. Not far along on a signpost was *Marita*. What was it to be? The simple trick? The bluff of all bluffs?

"So you know where you're going," Eloise said.

"Pasadena Farm, beyond Marita. Ever been there?"

"No."

"You won't be able to say that soon." He was going; in his head he'd known he could not keep away.

"Do you think your wife's there?"

Dawlish didn't speak.

Eloise said slowly: "I haven't known you for long, Pat, but I've known you long enough to be sure you won't just drive up to the farm, as Clay told you to, and wait to see what happens. Because it won't be worth waiting."

He didn't answer. They came to Marita, where there was less than a hundred yards between the first garage and the last. On the right and the left were the great patches of peach and orange trees, leaving dark green, sandy soil beneath them looking too barren to grow anything. Just beyond the village was the second turning to the right and on a nearby corner was a fruit stand gay with the colours of apples, oranges, pears and plums. A huge sign read: FRESH ORANGE JUICE, 15c. Dawlish pulled off the road just beyond the sign, and said:

"How would you like some orange juice?"

"As I can't get a real drink, maybe it's a good idea."

"Fine. Stay here." Dawlish got out of the car. No one else was near, except two young girls at the fruit stand. He went across and they crushed oranges, filled two large glasses and put in some ice chippings with a long-handled spoon. He carried the drinks back to the car. It wasn't cool but it was less hot there. Eloise was standing in the shadow of a tree; she had powdered, and looked almost cool, in one of her better moods, fear almost forgotten.

"That looks delicious, Pat."

"Doesn't it?" They drank. "It's possible that we're being watched by someone inside that fruit stand. Certainly by no one else. We aren't far from the peach farm. If you come with me, I think I'll have a better chance. You needn't come, you've still time to change your mind."

He sipped the juice, watching her all the time.

CHAPTER XXIV

PASADENA FARM

THE sign pointing towards Pasadena Farm looked so bright and new that it might have been freshly painted for them. Dawlish slowed down and then stopped, giving himself room to turn into the narrow dirt road along which the sign pointed. Eloise looked between the rows of peach trees and along the road which was little more than a track, although there were tyre marks which looked recent.

"If anything's certain, Clay won't be here," Eloise said.

"I don't think you know how badly Clay is worried."

"He wouldn't take the chance that you'd do what he said. No one else would do just that. He isn't able to imagine a man who says, 'I promise this' and goes ahead and does it. Not Clay. I don't think you've even started to understand Clay."

"I think he thinks one of two women could hang him and he'll take every risk that he has to, so as to stop them," Dawlish argued. "They've taken plenty of risks already. They've thrown away a perfect hide-out like Huni Canyon and one nearly as good in One Shoe. If you ask me, Clay's backing out. The thing he fears most is the blackmail. He'll never be safe while the blackmailer's alive."

"Maybe not," Eloise said.

Dawlish let in the clutch and turned along the narrow road. No one appeared to watch and no one followed.

"He wouldn't have burned One Shoe or taken the chance with Huni Canyon if he weren't. He doesn't need them again, he knew that when he used them this time. Whatever he's doing, he knows it's too hot for him to go on any longer. He has one worry, keeping in the clear himself. It's as simple as that."

Eloise said almost laughingly, "The man who knows he can never be wrong!"

"I like to hear you laugh," Dawlish said.

He knew what reason told her but didn't share her belief. He was curiously calm and almost buoyant. There might be no reason in the world why he should feel that way, but he did. He watched the trees for signs of men but there was none. The road twisted, and now they were out of sight of the main road. The rows of peach trees stretched out to the horizon in all directions. The sky was a pleasant blue now, with white fur for clouds, and the sting had gone out of the sun, the wind was no longer hot. He glanced at the speedometer and saw that they had travelled nearly a mile on the farm road; they travelled another and there was no change in the road, although they had crossed two others, each marked with a signpost telling them where to go; older signposts, weather-beaten but still easy to read.

Then they turned another corner and the house was in front of them, beyond a white gate which stood wide open.

• • • • •

It wasn't just another house. It was large. The frame walls had been freshly painted white, and it was almost too dazzling. There were laid-out grounds, a swimming-pool with two small white-painted huts near it, and on a stretch of lawn over which a sprinkler played gently were two blue and yellow umbrellas, giving shade to small tables and chairs. Flower-beds were rich in colour.

No one was in sight.

Dawlish drove on slowly, and the car rattled over a cattle guard of metal rollers. He pulled up in front of the house. When he switched off the engine he could hear the gentle swish of the water from the sprinkler; that was all. He didn't open the door. Eloise sat very still, looking at the front door as if expecting it to open at any moment. It didn't.

Dawlish said, "Perhaps they didn't expect us so soon." He got out, and looked behind him—and saw that the gates were closed. He turned his gaze away; Eloise hadn't noticed. They'd been closed by the touch of a switch when the car had crossed the cattle grid.

From here the fence looked higher and impregnable, like the wall of a prison. It ran all round the spacious garden. hidden here and there by bushes.

Nothing stirred. Dawlish stared at the clear water of the pool, which hardly rippled; the lines of green tiles at the bottom looked quite straight. The water seemed to invite him, had the heady effect of wine. Watching the house and the shaded windows, he went to the dressing-huts. There were swim-trunks and swim-suits hanging out to dry, towels, sandals.

It was as if whoever owned the place had got up and left, leaving everything as it was.

When he went back to the car, looking at that frowning wire fence, Eloise was standing up.

"Are there showers?" As if that mattered.

"Yes."

"I shall scream if I don't have a bathe."

"You scream," said Dawlish. He still had his coat on and the gun in the shoulder holster seemed heavy and made him hot; the smaller gun in his coat pocket weighted the coat down. He took Eloise's arm and led her towards the house. The buoyancy remained, but there was tension too. No one appeared when they walked up the four steps towards the front door; and that was ajar.

Eloise was very close to him.

He pushed the door open and stepped into a cool, dim hall. Doors stood open. He went towards the first and looked into a lounge with a long window; its venetian blinds were drawn up and through the slats he could see the pool, the lawns and the flower-beds. The furniture was modern, exactly right for a room like this. He went out and into the other downstairs room, and there was no one here. From each window he could see the fence and the closed gates. The kitchen was a white, tiled palace, and the only sound was the gentle humming of the refrigerator.

Eloise went to that, opened it, took out a small tin of orange juice, found a tin-opener in a drawer, then a tap with the words 'Iced Water' on it. She mixed drinks and they drank without speaking.

There were five rooms and two bathrooms upstairs. The place was luxurious, perfect, cool everywhere. In the bedrooms oddments of clothing lay about, but nothing he recognized. He reached the last door at the end of a narrow passage; it was closed; he tried the handle and found it locked.

Eloise said, "He's fooled us, but why should he do it this way?"

"Or he's just being cautious." Words didn't matter. The dynamo inside Dawlish began to thunder. He looked at the door and the keyhole; it would be easy to pick the lock. He gripped the handle tightly and put his shoulder to the door, thudded against it as Samson might have heaved at the pillars of the temple. The door groaned and creaked. Dawlish drew back, then lunged again and the door swayed open. He kept his balance, dropped his right hand to his pocket about his gun, but that was almost mechanical. He couldn't think, and his heart seemed to rise in his throat, his chest felt as if he could never breathe easily again.

It was a small bedroom, shaded like the rest. He reached the window in four strides and kept his hands steady as he raised the blind to get more light. Eloise stood like a statue in the doorway.

The room was empty, but Felicity had been here. There were Felicity's clothes. There, on the bedside-table, was a leather-covered photograph of Dawlish. There was her travelling clock, oddments he knew she had brought with her, all precious things.

But not Felicity.

• • • • •

Dawlish left Felicity's room blindly, then forced himself to think. He explored the passage. There was a bathroom opposite the bedroom door. He went in. Just outside was a tall tree; the only one near the house. It gave some cover from the grounds. Below was the roof of part of the house, the kitchen. Felicity had been within a few yards of a window from which she could have climbed. Dawlish turned away, then went from room to room, pulling up the blinds and looking out of the windows. Beyond the fence were the peach trees and beyond them more trees; there was nothing else in sight.

Silently, Eloise followed him everywhere. It was half past five when they reached the front door again, and the pool still beckoned.

"Why did they go?" she asked helplessly. "Why have they done this?"

"They'll come back."

"There are times when I could hit you," she said shrilly. "What makes you think you know?"

"Get into Clay's mind your own way. He would expect Morgan to be close behind me. He'd expect me to come but not just with you. He'd protect himself by being out of reach. But he'll have someone watching. When he's sure we've come by ourselves, he'll come back. Because while he's a chance to learn who's blackmailing him, he'll have to come."

She spoke with slow, reluctant agreement. "You could be right. How long will he wait?"

"I'd guess, until it's dark."

"Nearly two hours."

"Is that so long?"

"Pat, I don't think I can wait here, not for two hours. If it could have happened quickly, so that there was no time to think . . ." She broke off.

"Well, don't think. I'll go and get a drink. Then we could eat."

"Food would choke me."

"All right, I'll get a drink," Dawlish said. He went into the house, and into the big lounge where there was a cocktail bar in one corner. He hurried, took out Scotch and bourbon, soda and glasses, left them on the bar and went to the window. Eloise was walking towards the swimming-pool. That feeling that she had been fooling him had never been stronger, but she didn't seem in any hurry to get away. He went back for a tray, loaded it, found ice in a cold-box beneath the bar, chipped some and put it into a glass bowl. When he reached the verandah steps, she was on the other side of the pool. He followed her. She was looking right and left, as if certain that someone would appear, but no one did. He reached one of the tables beneath an umbrella, and put the tray down. She disappeared into a hut. He went quickly to the nearest section of the fence, took a key off his chain and tossed it against the wire. The tiny blue flame and the hiss of sound did not surprise him, just told him that there was no easy way out, this was a prison. He didn't like to think of what would happen to Eloise's nerve if she knew they were surrounded by a live-wire fence.

He hurried back as she came out of the hut, wearing a swimsuit with a pleated skirt which almost reached her knees, and a brassière top that was too tight. She was pushing her hair beneath a silver cap, and stood on the edge of the pool like that, as if she were anxious now only to draw Dawlish's gaze; but she didn't look towards him. She stood still for a moment, then put her arms out and her hands together, and dived in; she cleft the water with hardly a splash. He sipped and watched her as she swam lazily to the far end of the pool, and then back. She clutched the edge and laughed at him, as if the plunge had taken her out of fear.

"Come and help me out."

He went across to her, bent down, and took her wet hands. A moment later she stood in front of him, water dripping like pearls from her smooth skin. She dried her hands and face and then came across to the table, put the towel on a chair and sat down.

"Why don't you go in?"

"I haven't your nerve. They might be back before I expect them."

"It's wonderful in there."

"You go back. You're easy to watch."

She sipped her drink, and then shook the ice round and round in the glass.

"That's almost the first pretty thing you've said to me."

"I haven't felt in the mood for saying pretty things."

"I guess that's true," Eloise said softly. "You'll always know what it's like to have lived in hell, won't you? We have that in common. I've lived in terror of Clay for a year—hating him and yet compelled to stay with him."

"Compelled?" He spoke lightly, hoping to keep a mood of fear away.

"And now there's just a chance that I won't have to do that any longer," Eloise said. "I wish I knew what he was doing. I wish I could believe that you're right, and he's just waiting and watching to make sure that the police don't come this way. And when I've done hoping you're right, I wonder what will happen if you are—when he comes back. If *he* comes."

"He'll come."

She jumped up. "What are you? Half saint, half devil, fed by the tree of all knowledge?" She moved swiftly away and dived into the pool again with the same smooth competence, but this time she swam more swiftly, furiously. He envied her, but didn't get up. Nearly an hour had gone, and the sun was very low, it would be dark in less than an hour. The evening's magic touched the trees and the pool and the house, as it had touched the desert, and there was colour in the earth itself. He poured himself another drink and sat and smoked, until Eloise climbed out at the far end, without asking for help, and disappeared into the hut. She came out again within two minutes, a big towel round her, and she dabbed herself dry. She had taken off her cap and her hair fell in flaming glory to her shoulders. She seemed to ignore him. She dropped the towel and walked, slowly, lazily, out of sight, and when she had gone there was the picture of her golden beauty to remember; and the picture of Felicity, more than life size, to make his heart beat wildly again. Although it was cool, he felt himself sweating.

He found himself thinking, too; how to make the last call, to make Clay show his cards first.

Eloise came back, dressed. He mixed her another drink without speaking, and lit her cigarette. It was dusk; half an hour would see full darkness. There was no movement among the trees, except for the slight rustle of the wind, and none at all at the house.

"We could go inside," Eloise said.

"We can see better from here."

"I guess you'll please yourself," she said wearily.

Then she raised her head sharply, and Dawlish felt the tumult inside him grow fiercer. He turned his head. There was the sound of a car engine, drawing nearer. He stood up slowly, his right hand in his pocket about the gun. He took a step towards the road, and stopped because the car engine stopped. No other sound came for a while. The dusk shadowed the trees but the pale earth between them and of the road showed clear beneath a sky already decked with the brighter stars. Then he heard footsteps, approaching slowly, and believed that a woman was coming. He went nearer the road and the white posts of the gate, and he could hardly breathe, but his mind was forcing thoughts that warned him.

The gates opened; so there was outside control.

A woman came in sight and entered. The gates stayed open. Dawlish couldn't be sure but he believed that it was Felicity. He could hardly breathe. He walked slowly towards her, unaware of Eloise just behind him. Then the other woman stopped and raised her hands, and in that moment he was sure. There was a moment of unearthly silence, before she began to run towards him and he towards her—but as they drew nearer the warning inside him reached a screeching crescendo.

CHAPTER XXV

THE SECRET

FELICITY did not speak. There was only the sound of their footsteps, hers first on gravel and then on the grass; his first on the smooth surround of the swimming-pool and then also on the grass, and every step seemed filled with a flooding reality—and with that warning, that certainty of close and urgent danger. Inescapable?

Then they were together.

Dawlish felt the pounding of Felicity's heart beneath her breast, the soft warm fullness of her, the tension in the arms which were crushed against his chest. She strained towards him as if praying that they could merge into each other and become one and never be put asunder. Her breathing had the panting wildness of mingled desire and despair, unbelief fought with the knowledge that this was her man, alive and with a heart pounding wildly because they had found each other again.

The night, the stars, the house, the pool, the silent woman standing near, the trees, the quiet air, were all part of this reunion and yet apart from it. Then after a while he knew that she was crying and felt the burning of tears at his own eyes.

That was the beginning of reason.

He felt a slackening tautness, and his mind as well as his body became free—to think not simply of holding and having her but of what was to come.

"Pat," said Eloise. "Pat."

Her voice was quiet and frightened. Felicity did not seem to hear her, but Dawlish heard and made himself look round.

"Pat they won't let us go."

Felicity was crying but making hardly a sound; perhaps she hadn't heard. Dawlish moved so that his right arm was round her shoulders and her head was just in front of him, beneath his face, and fragrance came from her hair.

"They won't," Eloise insisted.

"Fel," said Dawlish in a voice quieter than the woman's, "we haven't much time. Listen to me, my darling, listen and try to answer." He paused, and her head lifted a little. "Fel, who brought you here, how many men? Tell me."

After an age, she found her voice.

"There were—two men."

"How far away?"

"Not far."

They'd brought her near in the car, and he hadn't heard the engine start up, so they hadn't gone away. They would be approaching on foot, and perhaps others were doing the same. The warning had been as real as it had been urgent. Now he could imagine the silent approach of men, closing in on the house. Clay wouldn't let them *live,* had made as sure as any man could that they would die before they left here; but first, Clay wanted what he believed they could tell him. That was the only hope. But when would they arrive and how would they attack? How would Clay try to terrify his victims into talking? All three had been standing close together for minutes which had grown to five or six.

"Eloise."

"Yes, Pat."

"Go slowly towards the car. Don't get in it yet."

"What——"

"Slowly. Don't hurry." He waited, and she began to move, but her reluctance was as clear as the stars above although she moved through darkness; but for the stars it was fully dark, and the only visible things were shadows. "Fel, my darling, we have to get away from here, we can't think about anything else yet. Have you seen Clay today?"

"Yes." Her voice was remote, far away.

"Here?"

"Yes."

"Do you know how he came?"

"There's an airstrip," Felicity said with the emptiness of unreality. "I came that way, too. By helicopter." Nothing mattered but the fact that they were together and that she was well, unhurt—except that gathering menace sheltered by the darkness, drawing closer, although it was impossible to guess from where it would come or how it would come. "I saw him arrive from my window. Well, a small 'plane landed and he arrived soon afterwards."

Her window faced south; he had stood on the spot where she had stood yet seen no gap in the trees; but there was the airstrip and knowledge of it helped him to think. Clay was on his way out, waiting only to make his final effort to keep himself safe from the law. Perhaps he knew he had gone too far now. The 'plane would be ready to take off when Clay reached it.

Felicity was still held within Dawlish's right arm, and he could feel her quivering. She knew as well as he that this was not the end, only the beginning of the end. The menace touched her as closely as it did him, nothing else could have kept her there, or put the emptiness into her voice. He hadn't seen her yet; not *seen* her.

"Have you heard them talking? Planning?"

"A little. Clay's being blackmailed. He said Bill Newton was a spy. I saw him push . . ." She broke off, and Dawlish did not harass her. She had to fight for words. "Then he caught me. He thought I was there to see Newton. He—he was going to burn me. I couldn't stand it, I just couldn't stand it. I said I didn't know a thing, but that you did."

That brought a blinding light of understanding. He almost squeezed the breath out of her.

"Yes, my darling. Go on."

Her voice was thick, as if she were crying.

"He was so sure I'd come to see Bill Newton. If I'd denied it any more he would have burned my—my breast. I said I'd just come to tell Newton *you* were coming. I knew you'd come. I hated myself for preparing a trap for you, but I couldn't bear it. I . . ."

He comforted her, calming her quivering body. When he spoke again it was very quietly.

"Have they said anything today?"

"No. They took me away from here early this afternoon, to a small house a few miles away. They didn't say anything when they brought me back, except that I must walk to the pool."

It hadn't occurred to her that she might take a chance then, run and get lost among the trees. So they had dulled her mind.

Soon an attack would come, but from where? The darkness was an ally, but Dawlish sensed that it would be treacherous. He turned and walked towards the car, just able to make out the shape of Eloise standing by it.

What would Clay expect him to do?

Get into the car and drive off. Clay would know him as the man who had leapt into that savage assault at the hut near the

Canyon; as a creature of impulse, who would batter his way through opposition, wherever it was. Yes, he could be sure that Clay expected him to do that, and would be on the road to meet him. The open gate invited him but there was no other way out, the fence made their prison.

He heard Eloise call:

"Why don't we get away? Why are we staying here?"

"Because he expects us to try to escape."

Felicity didn't ask about Eloise, just clutched Dawlish; but she was more herself, walking with greater freedom and her chin no longer drooped to her chest; the climax of relief had passed.

"How many roads are there from here, my darling?"

"Just the one, I think," she answered promptly. "Others lead from it, but there's only one road from the house."

That suggested that he might be right, that Clay was waiting for him to rush like a bull at a red rag, relying on his speed and brute strength.

They were ten yards from Eloise.

"I can't stay here any longer." Her voice was shrill, unsteady, "I'm leaving!" She opened the door of the car and Dawlish heard the sounds. "You ought to come, not wait here. It's driving me mad."

"It's doing that," Dawlish agreed softly. "That would be mad." But where did sanity lie? If he jumped that fence and began to walk through the trees towards the airstrip there was no way of being sure that he would reach it; he hadn't seen it, it might be half a mile or two miles away. The magnet was Clay—he was likely to be near, waiting for fear to drive them to confession.

Was there a way to use this sheltering darkness and defying its menace?

Then light killed the darkness.

It came from the pool, lighting beneath the water that he hadn't seen, green, red and blue, clear and betraying them, showing everything as if it were the light of day. Beyond it there was still the darkness, but the radius of light stretched as far as the house, passing the car, and beyond the sheds on the far side. The umbrellas and the tables showed up clearly and the flowers were touched with different hues.

Dawlish saw Eloise with her hand on the door of the car, and *saw* Felicity, startled, looking at the pool, clutching his arm more tightly. Then out of the surrounding darkness the first sound of danger came swiftly, the crack of a shot from the gates, which struck a wing of the car and made Eloise snatch her hand away.

Eloise screamed.

Dawlish did not move, just stood with his arm round Felicity's waist.

"Clay!" he roared.

There was no further shot, no audible movement; but Clay's voice came.

"You played it well, Dawlish, but it didn't win for you. I know that no one sent you, I know who put the black on me."

When he stopped, the silence seemed to quiver, killing hope.

"I did some hard thinking when I discovered Eloise made a deal with you. I've been to her place. Everything I wanted was there. She was the blackmailer. The bitch. She put me on to Newton, too, she named him."

Eloise screamed:

"I warned him to be careful! I warned him you were working in the Canyon. Yes, *I* did. I beat you, Clay, I fooled you. *I* did. While you were ordering me here, sending me there, while you thought you'd bought my mind as well as my body, I squeezed a fortune out of you. I made *you* afraid, I made you walk in fear. I always meant——"

A shot came from beyond the fence, breaking the shock of Dawlish's understanding.

Eloise the blackmailer. Eloise the cause . . .

It seemed to release Dawlish from an awful tension. He lifted Felicity off her feet and raced towards the steps. He heard Eloise behind him, then the car door slammed. Shots roared. As he reached the verandah the engine turned. Eloise drove towards the open gate and the sound of shots was clear above the engine. She drove towards death and for all he knew he was running into it. The door stood open and he saw no one. He put Felicity down, slammed the door and locked it; but there were other doors and windows.

"It's all right, Pat," Felicity said so quietly that he could hardly hear her voice above the shooting and the roar of the engine. "I knew it was a chance in a thousand. It's all right, my darling." In the darkness he couldn't see her, but her voice now had its own calmness. "All I really hoped was to see you again."

Into the silence there came a crash, rending, frightening; and then there was silence, there was no more need of shooting. Felicity turned towards the door but he grabbed her round the waist, pushed her towards the stairs.

"Your room," he said. "Wait for me there."

"Pat——"

"Wait for me!" he ran into the big lounge and switched on the light, could see the coloured glow from the swimming-pool but nothing else, no one approaching from the front. He took out his knife and slashed a cushion and the down filling spilled out. He snatched matches from his pocket, struck one, spent a precious moment sheltering it to get the flame steady, then held it to the filling; it began to blaze. From the doorway, Felicity saw what he was doing and ran towards the window, picking up a book of matches from a small table.

"Come away!" Dawlish roared.

She struck a match and held it beneath the linen drapes, waiting until they began to burn. The cushion was blazing and the flames were a foot high. Dawlish ripped other cushions and shook the filling out.

"*Come away!*"

Felicity swung from the window, her face bronzed in the light of the burning. Dawlish picked up small chairs and smashed them across his knee, laid them on to the fire; they began to spark and crackle. He moved towards the door, took Felicity and thrust her behind him. Gun in hand, he peered into the passage, and saw the man coming through a door opposite the lounge. He fired, and waited to see the man move out of sight; he heard a thump, as if a gun had fallen.

"Upstairs." He thrust Felicity towards the stairs and she ran up. A shadow appeared from the kitchen door, and Dawlish watched the door opening, then fired twice; the door slammed. He backed up the stairs. Halfway up he was safe from shooting except from the front door. He heard voices and he heard the crackling of the fire; firelight danced on the glass of pictures hanging in the hall and up the staircase wall. He reached the landing as the other door opened wider again. He fired at it twice, then turned to see Felicity halfway along the narrow passage leading to her room. He pulled a couch towards him and ripped the seat with his knife, tore down the drapes from the window, set them alight and dropped them on to the couch; everything was tinder dry. As the couch blazed he pulled it from the wall, stood it on end, and with the flames snarling at him pushed it down the stairs. It thundered as it fell and the flames were dulled for a moment. Near the foot of the stairs it jammed between the banisters and the wall, and flames shot yards into the air. Smoke crept about the hall, and the light was the light of an inferno.

He turned his back on it. Felicity was at the end of the passage. Dawlish thrust open the bathroom door. They stood looking at each other for a moment, then he seized her and his lips crushed hers—and he thrust her away, almost savagely.

"We'll stay here for a bit. We aren't far from the main road and houses. The fire will be seen, once it takes a good hold. When the others come, Clay will have to draw off his men. There's some cover by this window, when it gets too hot we can get out there, down on to the roof below. It gives us a chance." He stared into her eyes, searching for the signs of the ordeal and seeing some, but most were hidden, one thing was ringing in his mind. He meant as much to her as she meant to him, and if he had ever doubted it for a moment he now knew that she meant everything.

She could even smile.

"We may not get Clay yet," he said. "But if we can stay alive, we'll see him hanged." He pulled her towards him again. "What else do you know, Fel?"

The calmness was still in her.

"I saw Clay push Newton into the Canyon. I'd got up early and met Bill. He'd found out they were doing something crooked. I suppose that woman did tell him. He'd suspected it for a long time, but the day he and I went along the Canyon's rim, he knew for certain."

Dawlish asked, as if it mattered with the house burning beneath them and desperate men ready to make sure that they did not get out alive:

"What was it?"

"There's gold," Felicity said simply. "Clay's men have been mining it by night, just beneath the surface. Big rocks hid them. Bill wanted to see them come out, and be absolutely sure. He'd heard them talking, so had I, but wasn't quite sure where the place was. I left the hotel early and met him at the rim just after dawn, but didn't know that I was followed. He didn't expect me. I—oh, I just had to go. Clay appeared. Bill tried to save me, and Clay pushed him over. I hadn't a chance to get away."

"No," Dawlish said softly. "You never had a chance."

"I think they would have killed me," Felicity said, "but they thought I was in it, too. He'd told Clay you—you were Britain's ace detective! Bill knew what he was doing, he wanted to give me a chance and he gave it to me. You see, Pat, he knew about you, had heard a lot about you in Haslemere. You did a little job for M.I.5 at the camp where he was stationed, and someone built you up. He'd talked to me about it the previous day."

"Yes," Dawlish said.

"I've told you the rest. I couldn't face the red-hot irons he threatened me with. I told him I'd only come to tell Newton that you were coming. I had to make it sound convincing. I said you were working for someone over here in the States."

It was all so clear, so obvious, now. And all the time Eloise, out of her hatred, had blackmailed Clay, who thought that she was his as a dog might be his.

They fell silent, but through the quiet there was the roar of the fire below.

CHAPTER XXVI

THE BURNING

DAWLISH moved towards the window, his arm round Felicity's waist. It had always seemed hot, but this was a different heat. Each knew, without having to speak, that they would have to climb out now. Dawlish looked out into the lurid red glow where it met and overpowered the paler light from the pool. The tree gave some cover, but too little. He stood to one side but knew that he might be seen from outside, if there were men waiting to see; and where else would they be?

No one fired at him.

The far end of the house was ablaze, and nothing would ever put it out. There would be no chance of saving any of it. This end was farther from the flames than any other part; as he had planned. Smoke stung his nostrils and the roar of burning filled his ears. If everything were what it seemed to be, they could climb down safely. He watched for the sign of men and saw nothing—but he heard a new sound. It went through him like an electric shock. He felt Felicity's fingers tighten on his arm. The sound, once it began, was never-ending, a wailing siren so faint at first that he could have been wrong, but soon stronger and drawing nearer.

"We can wait five minutes more," he said.

The siren began to wail so loudly that he could picture it coming into sight; it didn't. Up and down, up and down, it was like the wail of a banshee. Why didn't it come? Wouldn't its coming drive away any of Clay's men who were ready to shoot? Was it safe to climb down; first to lower Felicity and then to go down himself? Compared with the climb into the Canyon, this was nothing.

Then the fire-engine swung through the gates with several men clinging to it. It slowed down and men jumped off and carrying the hoses ran towards the pool, as if they had known it was there. Some ran nearer the house. Dawlish leaned out of the window and roared at them to keep away from the fence. They seemed to understand; a man went running and stood guard at the gate. Another engine came, drawing a water-carrier.

There was still a chance that Clay's men were waiting and would shoot, even at the last minute, but no shot came. The firemen, flames leaping and spreading light on their steel helmets, came hurrying, carrying a ladder. There would be no need to climb down or to take risks. Felicity came closer to the window, men below wasted no words but ran the ladder up, and one came hurrying to help. Felicity climbed backwards out of the window, the man moved down but was ready in case she should fall. Dawlish watched her as she went down, face upturned set in a strange smile; radiant.

Why not? They had the world to laugh at?

He still scanned the nearer trees beyond the fence. No one appeared. He started to climb down. Had Clay's men been driven off by the arrival of the fire-engine? It was possible, it was even likely.

He kept looking over his shoulder, was halfway to the ground when he saw the movement he expected, just beyond the fence. He shouted, "Look out!" and jumped. He saw a flash among the trees but it did not show the face of the man who fired; the shot cracked. He heard Felicity call out as he landed, steadied himself and turned and raced towards the fence. Men shouted out behind him, he thought he heard Felicity running, turned and saw a fireman holding her.

He was a clear figure against the blazing house; all of them were. He watched for the next shot, sure that it would come; and it came yards away from the first. The bullet missed him. He turned and ran towards the spot, weaving right and left, getting closer to the fence which the man beyond believed gave him protection. He could see the man standing among the trees calm and still; he could imagine the gun in the steady hand. He saw flame spurt. He felt nothing but he pitched forward, his left shoulder down. As he hit the ground he kept his eyes open and watched—and saw the man much more clearly, gun raised, as if to send a last bullet into Dawlish's head before turning away. Dawlish fired. The shadowy figure moved abruptly; he fired again and saw the man fall. Dawlish got to his feet slowly, warily. Men were running behind him. In the distance another siren sounded. Then a searchlight from the first engine shone out, piercing the gloom among the trees, shining on Clay who was on the ground, struggling to get up, a gun in his hand.

Dawlish shot at the gun; it was like target practice. He saw the gun fall and Clay fall over it and lie crumpled, broken, beaten.

Then he became aware of other men among the trees, hurrying. He felt a streak of fear go through him like the blade of a knife. For one of the men was Morgan and he was very near the fence. Dawlish roared:

"Keep away, it's live, keep away!"

Morgan heard him, and stopped. They stood on either side of the fence, without speaking, until a fireman came running to say that the main switch had been found and the wire fence was dead.

• • • • •

Morgan walked with Dawlish towards the burning house. Hoses were playing on it but could do no more than keep the flames from devouring the outhouses. Men showed up dark against it, like Felicity. The men who had come with Morgan collected in a half-circle, as if to make sure that Dawlish didn't break and run; it seemed that he would never be free from the need for running, but he was free. Two of them carried the body of Trig Clay.

"No, we didn't know where you were coming," Morgan said. "But it wasn't so hard to trace a man of your size, friend, it just took time. We got as far as Marita, and did some inquiring. We learned about the house here and the airstrip, and we got around to finding out that the man who owned the place could be Clay, only he didn't call himself Clay. He had a woman here, too. We closed in from all directions, taking it slowly. We reckoned if we could cut him off from the airstrip, it would finish him.

"And it did," Morgan declared with quiet satisfaction. "By then he'd given up trying to force his men to attack you. You'd kicked them too hard too often. Once you'd started the fire and driven them off you had Clay beaten, but he wouldn't leave. He meant to kill you. Then we arrived, friend. Most of Clay's men didn't trouble to fight. They told us Clay was gunning for you." Morgan paused. "I'll tell you something, Dawlish. You had me scared."

They stopped in front of Felicity.

Morgan looked at her, as if trying to find out what made her the only woman in the world. It was not in beauty, for she was good to see but had none of the magnificence of Eloise. It was not in figure, for she was tall and slender, not deep-breasted. Was it in her eyes? They were grey-green, more grey than green, with a strange, almost unnerving calmness. Or was it a quiet spirit which the huge man reverenced?

She waited on Dawlish for guidance. Then Dawlish saw men walking from the narrow road, carrying a stretcher, with the ambulance behind, coming up to turn round. Morgan and Felicity turned to see what had caught Dawlish's eye, and driven everything else out of his mind.

Eloise lay on the stretcher.

Dawlish moved towards her slowly, and saw the firelight reflecting on her eyes; so she wasn't dead, she was conscious. For the first time since he had reached the Canyon he could think of her without thinking of Felicity. The men stopped and put Eloise down gently; Dawlish reached her. There was a sheet drawn up to her shoulders; her forehead and chin were bruised, her lips cut.

"How is she?"

"She's lucky to be alive," the man said. "But I guess she'll be lucky for a long time."

Dawlish grinned; that was suddenly easy. Eloise smiled up at him crookedly, painfully. Felicity drew level and Morgan was only just behind.

"You want to know something?" Eloise asked.

"Anything you care to tell me."

"I was going to tell you. I'd seen you break Clay up and I wanted you to finish him. I'd got all I wanted, I'd made life hell for him. He was everything I hated for the reason I told you and I looked for a way to hurt him. A lot of people wanted to know where he was getting his money, they weren't convinced it was all from the gaming tables. I found out. I blackmailed him. He was living each day as if it would be his last. But he was strong. He'd broken up the body of the one man I loved, and then you started to break his. It was fine. I was glad to help." She gave a queer, twisted smile. "I was sorry about Newton and your wife. I wanted to help. But in a way I was glad I'd made you come to break his body." She paused and her face twisted as if she were in sudden pain, but the smile soon came back wryly, meant for Dawlish alone.

"But I helped, didn't I? Tell me you couldn't have done this without me."

"It would have been impossible," Dawlish said. "You could have named Clay to the police, told them what you knew and had him caught. But that might not have led to my wife. You took quite a chance, Eloise." He bent down slowly, and kissed her lips, gently.

Eloise looked away from him for the first time, and towards Felicity. Her smile was something to see. The red of the fire was behind Felicity and Dawlish.

"You're his wife," Eloise said. "You ought to know something about him, and in case you don't I'm going to tell you. He's the biggest liar I know. It would have been im*poss*ible! He doesn't even admit that word's in the dictionary." She looked back at Dawlish. "Maybe he doesn't always keep his word. This time you have to make him. He promised to take me back to Europe with the two of you."

• • • • •

Dawlish spent a lot of time in Hollywood, lazing, marvelling; that after the first strange, hurtful yet magnificent days of new discovery of each other, Felicity could still be interested in shops, film studios, anything America had to show. They had both found time to visit Eloise daily, in hospital. They were at the hospital to take her away when she was discharged, and they took her straight to the home of Felicity's friends, in Beverly Hills, and weren't surprised when the thinnest man in the world with the most lined face stood up slowly from a garden chair and watched them get out of the car.

"Sheriff Morgan, I believe," Dawlish greeted solemnly. "I want you to meet my wife."

"So you get some things right," Morgan said. "I'm more happy to see you again than you'll ever believe, Mrs. Dawlish." He paused. "Hi, Eloise." Nothing would ever make him hurry. "I guessed you'd be anxious to know if we found anything in the Canyon, and what we found."

"You're even thinking straight as well as crooked," Dawlish marvelled.

"We found plenty," Morgan informed them. "The really clever men from Washington were with us, maybe that's why. That gold was so thick in the seam every hour they worked it made Clay a fortune. He'd been working it for some time, with Kramer in charge on the site. Clay often visited the Canyon, saying he liked being there. I'll say he did! He was the big shot but kept under cover, until Kramer sent word to a Las Vegas stooge Clay used, saying that Bill Newton was prowling a lot by night. Clay sent himself to handle that. It was Mrs. Dawlish's bad luck that she came at that time.

"From the moment you broke him up and made him mad, he did crazy things. You frightened him, I guess. He had to know who was after him. For all he knew Bill Newton was a private eye; and for all he knew you were aiming to muscle in. And he was paying out blackmail to someone he didn't know but who could tell the police he had some peculiar interest in the Canyon, and about two killings two years or so back."

"Have you evidence against the blackmailer?"

"Not enough to show to a jury," Morgan said. "No, sir. Some things aren't worth trying to prove. Not now, anyway. There wasn't much good in Trig Clay, friend, was there?"

"I don't know everything there was in Clay," Dawlish said. He looked at Felicity; he would never tire of looking at Felicity. "Think of the things he could have done to my wife, and didn't."

Morgan shrugged.

"Well, maybe. Look at the thing he would have done to Eloise if he'd not been stopped. Don't you go seeing good in the man just because you killed him, friend. One Shoe was burned with Eloise in it, on his orders. He had finished with the ranch and was destroying all his traces. I can tell you more. The gold was refined at Huni Canyon. He had two-three other places, including a shack in the redwoods. And if you like to know about small things, he had Mrs. Dawlish's car driven into a small canyon, where we found it wrecked." Morgan turned his small, bright eyes on to Felicity. "Mrs. Dawlish, ma'am, last time we met there was some kind of excitement, I didn't have a chance to tell you a thing. Now I'll tell you that you're married to the most stubborn cayuse on either side of the Atlantic, and maybe he's the toughest, too."

"As if I didn't know," Felicity said, and there was a catch in her breath.

Dawlish said lazily: "Your thinking won't get you far if it takes you in that direction, Sheriff. How about having a holiday—I mean, a vacation. Eloise is coming back with us. You wouldn't mind having him around, Eloise, would you?"

Morgan's eyes glowed.

"Not this time, but I'll take a rain check. Maybe Eloise will come back and report how you live in those old-fashioned parts, and I'll think about it then. Take good care of her, friend, she's quite a person."

THE END